MOURN THE LIVING

Other Five Star Titles by Max Allan Collins:

Butcher's Dozen

MOURN THE LIVING

a Nolan novel

Max Allan Collins

Five Star
Unity, Maine

A Nolan novel

This novel is a work of fiction. Names, characters, places, and incidents are either the product of the author's imagination, or, if real, used fictitiously.

Five Star Mystery
Published in conjunction with Tekno Books and Ed Gorman.

Cover photograph by Mary Smith

December 1999

First Edition, Second Printing.

Five Star Mystery Series.

The text of this edition is unabridged.

Set in 11 pt. Plantin by Rick Gundberg.

Printed in the United States on permanent paper.

Library of Congress Cataloging-in-Publication Data

Collins, Max Allan.
Mourn the living : a Nolan novel / by Max Allan Collins. — 1st ed.
p. cm. — (Five Star mystery series)
ISBN 0-7862-2211-5 (hc : alk. paper)
I. Title. II. Series.
PS3553.O4753 M68 1999
813′.54 21—dc21 99-045469

To the memory of Richard Yates—
who read this book
and told me I was a writer

A MOURNFUL INTRODUCTION
by the author

This novel was written around 1967 or '68, and is—in a sense—the first book in the Nolan series. But the first Nolan novel to be published was *Bait Money* (1973); and, as of this writing, five more books about the character have appeared over the years—most recently *Spree* (1987).

While Nolan has been inactive since, readers frequently inquire about his future; this novel, obviously, refers to his past, but perhaps those same readers will be pleased to encounter this "new" Nolan tale. From time to time, Hollywood has expressed interest in my thief and most recently an Italian company made serious cinematic noises; and I'm currently considering making my own independent film based on one of the novels. So I'm pleased to have this opportunity to bring Nolan's first adventure, at long last, into book form.

Written during my undergrad years, *Mourn the Living* was set aside when an editor suggested that he would like to see either certain rewrites (with which I did not agree) or the author's next book. I followed the latter course, figuring that *Mourn* would be published later on; but the subsequent series initiated by *Bait Money* differed from this first novel—among other things, Nolan aged ten years and acquired a youthful protege, Jon. Also, times had changed so rapidly that the novel's hippie-era time frame, so topical when I'd written it a few years before, seemed hopelessly dated.

It may sound unlikely, but I had forgotten about the book—at least in terms of it being a commercial property—until Wayne Dundee interviewed me for his fine small-press magazine *Hardboiled*. In the course of the interview, I mentioned the existence of *Mourn the Living* to Nolan fan Wayne, who expressed an interest in serializing it in *Hardboiled*.

So, twenty years after the fact, I found myself doing the necessary line-editing on the first Nolan novel. Too much time had elapsed for me to undertake any major rewriting. While the novel was recognizably mine, I realized I was a different writer, several decades down the road; and, like any good editor, I attempted to respect the wishes and intent of the young writer who wrote it. Now—another ten years or so having managed to slide by—Ed Gorman has been kind enough to inquire about collecting the serialized novel into this volume.

I hope readers will enjoy meeting the younger Nolan, sans Jon, in his first recorded adventure. As for the time period of the book being dated, I am pleased that enough years have gone by for me to present it, unashamedly, as a period piece.

My thanks to Wayne Dundee, for nudging me and giving *Mourn* an audience at last; to Ed Gorman, of course; and to my wife Barb, who patiently transferred the moldy, water-damaged manuscript onto computer disc for my editing.

PROLOGUE

The Nolan problem bothered Frank Rich, but there was a brighter side to the unpleasant coin: he'd been able to bring his mistress into his home for the first time.

Rich shifted nervously in bed, the sheet wet with his uneasiness, causing his brown-tressed bed partner to groan in displeasure at his restless turning, tossing.

"Am I bugging you, Nance, hon?"

She pulled the covers up and over her head and answered his question by peeping one runny mascaraed eye above them, rolling it round as though she were a comic in blackface. Then she gave him another groan and turned over on her stomach, apparently wishing she'd never traded those second-rate clubs she used to sing in for the bed of an insomniac.

"Sorry, hon," Rich soothed, patting the blankets where they sheathed her well-formed backside.

"Get to sleep, Frankie," she growled, "okay?"

"Sure, hon, sure."

Damn her, he thought. An empty-head like her didn't understand, couldn't understand a thing like Nolan.

Nolan.

Rich shifted again, feeling weak-gutted and foolish that the mere name of a punk like Nolan could run a chill across his spine. He had just closed his eyes and blanked his mind for the *n*th time when a knock at the bedroom door shot him out of bed like he'd been jabbed with a needle.

He shouldn't have jumped, he knew he shouldn't have, he knew it would be Reese. Reese, the man he had stationed downstairs in the library, Reese coming up to make his hourly report.

"Yes, Reese," he said, his voice surface-cool. "How's it going?"

"Dull, Mr. Rich. No sign of nothin'." Reese was big, like a medium-sized barn, and he was much tougher than his smooth pink facial complexion and much smarter than his baby blue, lamb-dropping eyes. Rich had confidence in Reese's knowing when and when not to make use of the object which caused the slight bulge beneath the big man's left shoulder.

"That's fine, Reese, we want it dull, don't we?"

"You sure you want me to keep comin' up on the hour like this?"

"Yes, Reese, it's best you do. This way I know you're still down there, alive and well."

Reese glanced over toward the double bed where Nance was sitting up, the pinkness of her making a pleasing contrast against the sheer blue nightie. She was looking pretty and looking pretty disgusted.

Reese said, "You ah, you're sure I might not be breakin' in on somethin' . . . personal?"

Rich forced a smile. He liked Reese, but the man thought too much. "No chance of that. Just go on back downstairs, Reese, and keep an eye open for anything out of the ordinary."

"Yes, Mr. Rich."

Rich closed the door on Reese and went back to the bed. He stood before it momentarily, then turned away, starting toward the door.

From the bed Nancy looked up, her sleep-filled eyes prying themselves open. She said, "Where you going, sugar?"

"To the can, hon, don't worry about me, just get some sleep."

"Brother . . . this Nolan must be a pretty damn tough character to shake you up this way."

Rich's face reddened, his hands clenched into fists. "Why the *hell* don't you just *shut your mouth* and go to *sleep?*"

Then, explosion past, the blood ran from his face and the fists became hands again. He smiled shyly, like a kid who's just said his first bad word, and said, "I'm sorry."

Nancy said nothing.

Rich's face hung. "I'm sorry, hon, really I am. I wanted these few days here at the house to be a nice change for you from all the . . . well, you know, secrecy. I realize how tired you must be of sneaking around all the time. When this Nolan thing came up, I finally had a legit sounding excuse to get the wife out of town for a while. You got to admit it was a good excuse."

"Only it's not an excuse," she pouted. "First you tell your fat old hag that it's too dangerous for *her* to stick around, then you invite *me* over. I guess that shows how much concern you have about my welfare."

"Hon!" Rich was exasperated. "Don't get upset just because I'm acting a little jumpy! There's no chance at all of this Nolan showing up around here. He'll try for the casino, or maybe one of the offices. Not here."

"Sure. That's why you been having Reese share our evenings."

Rich started to answer her, then decided against it. He turned away and went to the door and left the room.

In the bathroom Rich stripped down and appraised himself in the full-length mirror on the back of the door.

He thought he had a damn fine build for a man past fifty:

strong legs, trim waist, solid chest. There were some wrinkles, sure, and a little sag here and there, but a lot of men years younger, he felt confident, would trade him bodies gladly. Still had a touch of tan left, too, from that two-week summit conference with the Boys in Miami last summer.

Only his face didn't jibe with the rest of his youthful image, and of that he was well aware.

His face hadn't looked so bad to him three days before, when the Nolan threat had as yet to rise up. But now, now he looked at it and found things he hadn't noticed before. Like deathly pale skin, puckered with dry wrinkles, scattered with an occasional liver spot. And his hair, which only a few days before had seemed to him a distinguished premature gray, now looked a stark white, setting off the new oldness of his face.

Ridiculous!

In three days?

He wouldn't even think about it.

But Rich rubbed his hand over his chin (the stubble of his beard wasn't starting to grow in gray, now, was it?) and he knew that Nolan posed the kind of threat that could age a man, as they said, overnight.

Rich stepped into the shower stall, turned the faucet on both hot and cold, mixing the spray to an even lukewarm, and thought about the years he'd spent working his way up the ladder in the Boys' organization to get into this nice home in Cleveland, Ohio. Six and a half years he'd spent in Chicago, directly under the tight rein of the brothers Franco. Charlie and Sam Franco, along with Lou Goldstein, were the Boys, the three men who controlled the Chicago syndicate.

Rich soaped himself, adjusted the water just a bit warmer, and reflected on those six and a half years with the Boys, most of it spent working in various small casinos, and, toward the end, supervising the bookmakers. Then five more years he spent as Vito's second-in-command in Pittsburgh. Finally, for the past three years, he'd had his own set-up here in Cleveland, though still tied to the Boys. His operation wasn't a big one, but it was big enough to suit him: the apex of a career of hard, dedicated work in the none too safe business world of narcotics, gambling, prostitution, unionizing, and, well, other consumer services.

And now an obstacle: Nolan.

That damn renegade hood. Rich had hardly believed his ears when he'd heard that the Boys had set a price tag of a quarter mil on that punk's head.

Of course, Rich only knew of Nolan, had never met him. When Nolan had started working for the Boys in the Chicago operation, managing clubs for them, Rich was already with Vito in Pittsburgh. But Rich knew Nolan about as well as one man can know another second-hand.

He knew that Nolan was an ex-employee of the Boys, and had submitted his resignation in bullets, taking care of Sam Franco and two bodyguards when he did. Knew that for the past few years Nolan had been traveling around looting and generally tearing hell out of the organization's key operations.

Rich turned off the shower, slipped into a terry cloth robe to sop up the moisture.

He couldn't, wouldn't let the Nolan thing shake him. Nolan was only one man and, by reputation at least, a man who worked alone. He would hit some of Rich's sources of revenue, maybe, but he wouldn't think to hit Rich at home. Would he?

Three days before, when the rumor had filtered through his grapevine to him that Nolan was in Cleveland, Rich had moved what capital that was on hand and not in banks to his own wall-safe at home. For various reasons, reasons primarily concerned with matters of federal and state income tax, this money was not banked but kept on hand by the local operation till the Boys sent in a bagman from Chicago to pick it up once a month.

Now, forty thousand of this cash was downstairs in Rich's wall-safe, and Reese or someone like him had been serving guard duty on it ever since its arrival.

Rich got back into his pajamas. He hadn't thrown the case of nerves yet, but he felt a little better; he just didn't like thinking about what the Boys would do to him if he let Nolan lay hands on their money. He was half-way down the hall to his bedroom when he heard the noise.

It wasn't a very loud noise, just loud enough: a solid substantial *thump*.

Rich scrambled into the bedroom and got his .32 out from a dresser drawer near his pillow. He didn't bother Nancy; she was rolled over the other way, asleep.

He crept down the stairs and stood silently at the bottom for a while, facing the stately ivory-white double doors leading to the library, where waited the wall-safe and the forty thousand dollars.

"Reese?"

No answer.

"Reese?"

Rich opened the doors quickly, quietly, and entered holding the .32 in close to him, like an extra appendage. Trembling, he darted his eyes around the room.

There was no one in the library except Reese, who was stomach-down spread-eagled in the middle of the floor, like an X marking the spot. Rich went over to him, bent down. Reese wasn't dead, but from the looks of the back of his head—freshly red and a shade caved in—he wouldn't be waking up for a while.

Rich glanced over toward the wall where the picture of his fat wife Lily hung over the wall-safe. No sign of disturbance, outwardly at least.

Shaking badly now, Rich struggled out to the hall again and opened the front door. He wondered why his watchdog, a large German Shepherd, hadn't let out the usual howl he bestowed on visitors, friendly or otherwise. Then he noticed, looking out across the forty yards of lawn between him and the gate, the outline of the dog in the moonlight. The dog was lying still, but not dead, he was breathing too hard for that. Drugged apparently, Rich decided, and at any rate, out as cold as Reese.

He made his way back into the house, into the library. He shut the double doors behind him, looked around the empty room and felt a wave of calm wash over him.

Nolan had been and gone!

Obviously!

Rich smiled and reconstructed it. Nolan had come and tried to make Reese open the safe, and Reese, of course, hadn't known the combination. Then Nolan had heard the footsteps upstairs coming down, and, knowing that someone would be on the way with a gun, Nolan had made a hasty retreat! Rich breathed easily, allowed himself a smile.

Relaxed now, Rich headed for his wife's portrait, pushed it aside and opened the safe.

All the money was there.

All forty thousand.

So, Rich thought, he'd been right: the bigtime punk named Nolan had failed.

And Rich laughed.

"Something funny?"

Rich whirled, swinging the .32-filled hand around to meet the sudden threat imposed by the strange cold voice from behind him. But a massive rock of a fist smashed into his face and Rich felt himself going down like a sack of grain, and as consciousness began to leave him, he felt his hand go fish-limp around the .32. The little revolver dropped harmlessly to the floor, and so did Rich.

The tall, mustached, large-boned intruder reached into the opened safe and in one sweeping motion emptied its contents into the open mouth of a satchel. He closed the satchel, stepped over Rich and walked out of the library.

In the hall Rich's mistress was standing at the foot of the stairs, her pretty mouth wearing a wry lemon twist for a smile.

"Well?" she asked.

He opened the satchel, counted out five crisp thousand dollar notes and handed them to her. She took them and folded them into a neat, small square.

He leaned over to her, kissed her lightly.

"Thanks, Nance."

"Any time, Nolan."

ONE

1

The manager of the Motor-Inn looked across his desk at Nolan and said, "I hope your stay in our city is a pleasant one, Mr. Webb."

Nolan nodded and waited for his room key.

The manager smiled, and the smile was like a twitch in the middle of his florid face. "Will you be staying in Dallas long, Mr. Webb?"

Nolan didn't like questions any better than he liked smiles that looked like twitches. He dug into his pocket and came up with a twenty, traded it for his room key and shut the manager off like a TV. Then he lifted his suitcase, hefted the two clothes-bags over his arm and walked out of the motel office.

Once outside in the dry late afternoon air, he glanced down at the number on the key: 16. Good. That would be on the far side of the building, away from the highway and damn truck noise.

In his room he hung the clothes-bags in the closet and found a rack for his suitcase. He laid open the suitcase and took out a bottle of Jim Beam, unopened, a long-barreled .38 Smith & Wesson, unloaded, and a box of shells, half-empty. He ripped the virginal white seal from the mouth of the Jim Beam and carried it by the throat into the can, leaving the .38 and box of shells on the nightstand by the bed as he went by.

He tore the white wrapper off one of the bathroom drinking glasses and poured it half-full with whiskey, then turned on the faucet and added an afterthought of water.

He walked over to the bed, sat down and emptied the glass while filling the .38 with shells. He laid the loaded revolver back on the nightstand and rubbed the heels of his palms over his eyes. He was beat, washed-out; but he didn't feel particularly on edge, which was a good sign.

Maybe he was getting used to the idea of having a quarter-million-dollar price tag on his head. Or as used to it as anybody could get. After all, it had been a matter of years now, since the Family put out that open contract on him, with its promise of a 250 G payoff to anybody who could make the hit.

A quarter of a million was some kind of record, he supposed. Valachi had only rated a 100 thou. But then all Valachi had done was talk: the Family complaint against Nolan represented a complex blend of personal rage and monetary loss. And Nolan wasn't sitting in prison, his damage done—he was at large, his head packed with inside knowledge—not to mention he was looting key operations as only an insider could loot them.

Nolan's smile was almost non-existent as he reached for the phone on the nightstand. Before coming to Dallas for a short breather, Nolan had hit the Family's Cleveland branch for thirty-five thousand. Now he had to get the money safely banked in the Dallas account of "Earl Webb." He dialed the number of his local contact, a lawyer named M. J. Lange who for ten percent would gladly handle the cash for his client.

"Let me go back over it, Mr. Webb," Lange's voice said. "Tomorrow in the mail I'll get a key. The key will open locker 33 at the Greyhound Bus terminal, and in the locker will be a blue athletic bag. In the bag's the capital."

"That's about it," Nolan said. "Set?"

"Yes, Mr. Webb. One thing more . . ."

Nolan juggled the receiver on his shoulder as he lit up a cigarette. "What's that?"

"Sid Tisor's been after me to get in touch with you. He's phoned me long distance every night for a week and a half, and he sounds desperate. Wants you to call him. Says it's life or death."

"M.J., you know I don't want to screw around with anybody directly hooked to the Family."

"Well, I thought it best I pass it on to you. From what I hear, Tisor's made a clean break. Retired four or five months ago."

"Don't give me that crap. Nobody breaks clean from the Family. Sid is Charlie's damn *brother*-in law. How do you retire from that?"

"As I said, I'm just passing it on to you. He told me he did you a favor once."

Nolan ground out the freshly lit cigarette in disgust. "Did he leave a number? Goddamn him."

The lawyer fed Nolan the number.

"Didn't he leave an area code?"

"Oh yes," Lange said, "here it is. 309."

"Okay, M.J. Take care of that little blue bag, now."

"Of course, Mr. Webb."

Nolan slammed down the receiver.

Great, he thought. 309 was an Illinois area code. Close to the heat. That was all he needed.

Nolan glanced down at the bed and considered diving in. He hadn't slept well on the trip—he could never sleep well on a bus—and he needed the rest.

Then he dialed 1, area code 309, and Tisor's number.

Soon he heard, "Hello, Sid Tisor speaking."

"Hi, Sid."

"Nolan? Is that Nolan?"

"Yeah."

"How, uh, how about a favor for an old friend?"

"Maybe."

"I hear you been chipping away at the Family."

"Any complaints?"

"None. Didn't you hear I retired? As a matter of fact, the favor I want to ask of you could net you maybe forty thousand of the Family's money."

"What the hell are you thinking, Sid? When the Family lets a man retire, they trust him to keep his nose out of their business."

"Don't worry about them. They got faith in me."

"They got faith in nothing and nobody. How do you know they don't have your phone tapped?"

"They don't . . . why would they?"

"Life or death. Whose, Sid, mine?"

"Nolan, I got good reason to risk this."

"You had better."

"You remember Irene?"

Nolan said he did. Irene was Sid's daughter. Sid's wife Rosie had died in childbirth with Irene, and Sid had raised the child by himself. When Nolan had last seen Irene she'd been fourteen. Since then Tisor had sent her off to college somewhere. She'd be around twenty now.

"She's dead, Nolan."

"Oh."

"I think maybe she was murdered."

"That the reason you got ahold of me?"

"That's the reason."

"Where you living now?"

"Peoria—the boonies."

"The Family ever send anybody around to check on you?"

"Not once."

"It's a big risk for me, setting foot in Illinois."

"I know it is, Nolan."

"I haven't been in Illinois since the shit hit the fan."

"I know."

Neither one of them said anything for a while. Then Tisor said, "Will you come?"

"Yeah."

Nolan slipped the phone onto the hook and said, "Goddamn you, Sid."

It might be an okay score, but Sid always tended to exaggerate, and that forty G's he had promised might turn out closer to four C's. And Illinois wasn't the safest place in the world for you when every greaseball out of Chicago knew your face and knew it was worth a quarter million.

Nolan said, "Shit," and lit up another cigarette.

He didn't really give a fuck about Sid or his dead kid, but Nolan owed Sid, from the old days.

And Nolan paid his debts.

2

It took four buses to get to Peoria.

Nolan took rear seats on each of them and always tried to avoid attracting attention, and he was successful, but only with the men: from women he drew stares like flies around something dead.

There was nothing particularly striking about his clothing, just a blue banlon shirt and lightweight tan pants suited to the Texas weather, and a blue plaid woolen parka he was carrying to meet the already cooling Illinois climate. But when he stood, he stood six feet that seemed taller, a lean, hard man with muscular bronzed arms that a young woman who sat by him on the third bus had brushed against a few more times than the law of probability could allow. His thick desert-dry brown hair had begun to gray, and his angular, mustached face was deeply lined, making him look every one of his forty years. Behind black-framed, black-lensed sunglasses were gray eyes that kept a cold, close watch on everything.

On the final bus a lady of about sixty sat next to him and tried to small-talk him, but Nolan didn't small-talk easily. She seemed relieved when they at last reached Hannibal, which was her stop. She looked exhausted from an hour of making conversation with herself.

As she rose from her seat, she gave him the matronly smile of a professional grandmother and said, "Hannibal's a fascinating place, you know. Mark Twain was born here."

Nolan made an attempt at being pleasant, since she was getting off. "He wrote books, didn't he?"

She shook her head and waddled off the bus, boarding almost immediately a touring bus bound for Tom Sawyer Cave.

Nolan fell asleep for a while and woke up as the bus was passing a sign which should have read "Hello! Welcome to Illinois!" but somebody had removed the O in hello.

He closed his eyes and leaned back and rolled his past around in his mind for a few minutes.

Nolan had begun as a bouncer in a night club on Rush Street in Chicago. In a few years he climbed to manager. He was, of course, working for the Family; and the Family was grooming Nolan for bigger and better things.

At the head of the Family were "the Boys": Charlie Franco, Sam Franco and Lou Goldstein. Charlie and Sam were president and vice, while Lou held down the treasurer post. Their "outfit" was a multi-million dollar enterprise dealing in gambling, prostitution, unionizing and narcotics, among other consumer services, tied in with but largely independent of the New York mob families.

Nolan reached behind him and got his cigarettes out of the pocket of his parka. He lit one up and glanced out the bus window. He saw some crows picking at a scarecrow in a field and he thought of Sam Franco.

Sam Franco had been largely responsible for Nolan's promising future in the organization. Nolan hated the man on sight, which was natural since even Sam's brother Charlie referred to Sam as "the skinny little bastard" more often than not. But Sam was one of the Boys, so Nolan didn't advertise his feelings. And Sam, who tended to like young men more than young women, kept his admiration for Nolan platonic, because Nolan wasn't the type of man you made passes at, even if you were one of the Boys.

So for the next year and a half things ran smoothly. Nolan moved up in the organization, thanks to Sam, and Nolan kept on hating Sam's guts in silence, and everybody got along fine until Nolan met the girl.

The Illinois cornfields, already patched with snow, flashed in the bus window by Nolan's seat. He stared out the window and tried not to think about her. He didn't like thinking about her.

She was a nice girl, a very nice girl in spite of the fact that Nolan convinced her to spend the night with him during the first week of their acquaintance. She spent the night with him for two months. She had reddish blond hair, the high-cheekboned beauty of a model, an excellent body and was extremely quiet. All in all, she was everything Nolan wanted in a woman.

But she was something else, too, something Nolan didn't want: she was a cop.

Sam Franco called Nolan in for a special meeting the day after it became known that the girl was jane law. Sam informed Nolan that the girl would have to be removed. Nolan informed Sam that he had already told her to pack her things. What he did not tell Sam was that he too was packing his things, and would take off with her as soon as this blew over.

Sam said, "You're going to have to ice her."

"I can't do that, Mr. Franco."

"I'll tell you what you can and can't do! Now, this is your fucking mess, clean it up!"

"No."

"Ice the bitch, Nolan. That's my final word."

But Nolan's final word had been no, and he meant no. He didn't kill the girl.

Someone else did.

Nolan found her the next day, in his apartment, floating face up in his tub. The tub was overflowing with water turned pink from blood.

She'd been beaten first, to near-death, then drowned. Little of her beauty in life had been retained in death.

The emotional outlet Nolan knew best was violence, and he spent the next twenty minutes demolishing the apartment. He reduced all the furniture to rubble and smashed his fists through its plasterboard walls. When he had calmed down enough to think, he went down to the lobby of the apartment building to use the pay phone, since he had torn his own phone from the wall.

"This is Nolan, Mr. Franco."

"Yes, Nolan." Franco's voice exuded fatherly patience.

"Mr. Franco," he said, his voice even, his hand white around the receiver, "you were right about the girl. I want to thank you for . . . letting me avoid the dirty work."

"That's quite all right, Nolan," said Sam. "Come on over and we'll talk business."

Nolan went to Sam's penthouse office on Lake Shore Drive where he found Sam at his desk, enjoying the view of Lake Michigan out the picture window.

"Nice view," Nolan said.

Sam turned in his swivel chair, said, "Oh hello, Nolan. Yes, it is a nice view, particularly in May, when . . ." Sam had begun to get up.

"Don't get up, Mr. Franco," Nolan said, and Mr. Franco sat back down, two bullets from Nolan's .38 in his chest.

The first man through the door caught a bullet in the stomach, the next one through got his in the head. The odds were good that Nolan had gotten the girl's killer because the two men he had shot were Sam's personal bodyguards and had taken care of most of Sam's unpleasant chores.

Nolan waited for everyone to die, watching the doorway to see if anyone else wanted to join the party. When no one did, Nolan turned to the wall-safe opposite Sam's desk. His mouth etched a faint line of a smile as he twisted the dial to the proper combination: a few weeks before he'd been in the office for a conference and had watched carefully as Sam opened the safe. As Nolan had been storing away the combination for possible future use, Sam had boasted its being too complicated for anyone but a Franco to master.

Nolan emptied the safe's contents into a briefcase and walked out into the outer office, where Sam's secretary was crouching in the corner, waiting for death. Hauling her up by the arm, Nolan used her as a shield to get safely out of the building and into a cab, the .38 in her back making her a willing if not eager accomplice.

The police noted that the incident marked Chicago's fourth, fifth and sixth gangland slayings of the month, and promptly added them onto the city's impressive list. The Boys kept Nolan's name out of it (the secretary Nolan had used as an escort ended up describing him as short, fat, balding and Puerto Rican) because of the pains Nolan could cause them if he ever chose to reveal his knowledge of their organization's inner workings to the authorities. The Boys' benevolence, however, ended there.

Charlie and Lou, shocked to see bloodshed come so close to their personal lives, placed the quarter million on Nolan's head before Sam's body had even cooled.

Nolan had taken his twenty-thousand dollar bankroll, compliments of Sam's wall-safe, and headed for a friend's place, where he holed up two weeks, waiting for the heat to lift off Chicago. The friend who hid him out was named Sid Tisor.

Nolan looked out the bus window and watched the sun go down. He closed his eyes and waited for Peoria.

3

Tisor was waiting for Nolan at the bus station, asleep behind the wheel of his Pontiac, a blue year-old Tempest. Nolan peeped in at him. Tisor was a small man, completely bald, with unwrinkled pink skin and a kind face. His appearance hardly suited his role of ex-gangster. Nolan opened the car door, tossed his suitcases in the back, hung up his clothes-bags and slid in next to Tisor. He placed his .38 to Tisor's temple and nudged him awake.

"Nolan . . . what the hell . . ." Though the .38 barrel was cold against Tisor's skin, he began to sweat.

"Sid, we been friends a long time. Maybe too long. I'm worth a quarter million dead and you're still on good terms with the Boys. If you're part of a set-up to get rid of me, tell me now and you got your life and no hard feelings. If I find out later you're fingering me, I think you know what you'll get."

Tisor swallowed hard. He'd never heard Nolan give a speech like that before—he'd never heard more than a clipped sentence or two from Nolan at a time. Never in the ten years he'd known the man.

Tisor said, "I'm with you, Nolan. I don't have any love for Lou or Charlie or any of the bastards."

Nolan's mouth formed a tight thin line, which was as close to smiling as he got. "Okay, Sid," he said, and put the gun away.

Tisor turned the key in the ignition—it took a couple tries as the weather had turned bitter cold a few days before—and got the Tempest moving. He wasn't mad at Nolan for the stunt with the .38; he'd almost expected it.

Nolan said, "I haven't had much sleep, Sid. Take me to a motel, nothing fancy, but I want the sheets clean."

Tisor said, "You're welcome at my place. I got two extra beds."

"No. I'll stay at a motel."

Tisor didn't argue with Nolan. He drove him to the Suncrest Motel. He let Nolan out at the office and waited for three minutes while Nolan got himself set with a room. Nolan came back with key 8, which put him in a little brown cabin close to the end. There were ten cabins, stretched out in a neat row. Nolan walked to his and waved at Tisor to follow him.

Nolan started unpacking his clothes as soon as he got inside the cabin. Tisor said, "You want me to leave now?"

"Wait a minute. We'll grab some food at the diner across the road. But no talk about your problem till I've had a night's sleep."

Tisor again didn't argue with Nolan. He was used to putting up with the ways of the man. He knew Nolan's mind was his own and it was no use trying to change him. He would just go along with him and everything would work out all right.

The diner was boxcar style, and the two men took a postage-stamp table by a window. The place was cheap but clean, which was all it took to please Nolan. Tisor ordered coffee, Nolan breakfast.

"You were smart to get scrambled eggs," Tisor said. "Breakfast's always the best thing a diner serves."

"Right."

Damn you, Nolan, Tisor thought. Why is conversation such a task for you, you goddamn hunk of stone?

"You care if I ask you what you been doing the last six years or so?"

Nolan lit a cigarette. "Go ahead."

Tisor leaned over the table and whispered. "What's this I been hearing about you robbing the Boys blind? I hear they can't wipe their ass without Nolan's stole the toilet paper."

Nolan decided he might as well tell Tisor everything, so he'd have it out of the way—Tisor would hound him till he got it all, anyway.

"It started," Nolan said, "with them chasing me. They sent guns wherever I went. Mexico, Canada, Hawaii. Didn't matter."

"You ran."

"Sure I did. At first."

"At first?"

"Running gets tiresome, Sid. The first month I ran. After that I took my time. I knew the Boys, knew how they thought. Knew their operations. So when my original bankroll of twenty G's ran out, I went back for more. Looted any of the Boys' operations that were handy."

Their food came and they shut up till the waitress laid the plates down and left.

"How do you work it?"

"Huh?" Nolan said. He was eating.

"When you loot 'em. How do you work it?"

"Quick hit, planned a day or so in advance. Just me. Once in a while outside help, on a full-scale operation. Lots of pros working free-lance these days. Not even the Family controls professional thieves. Not many pros are afraid to help me, not with the money that's in it."

Tisor didn't bother Nolan any more. Now that Nolan had

his food and was eating, he wouldn't like to be bothered.

Tisor sipped his coffee and thought about his cold, old friend. What balls the guy had! Nolan had some stones bucking odds like that. And the hell of it was, if he kept moving, Nolan just might be hard enough a character to beat the Boys at their own game.

When both had finished, they got up from the table, Nolan paid the check and Tisor tipped the waitress a quarter. The two men walked out into the raw night air and waited for an opening to jaywalk back across the highway to the motel.

Tisor stood with his hands in his jacket pockets, watching his breath smoke in the chill, while Nolan got his key out and opened the door to the cabin. Nolan did not invite Tisor in.

He said, "See you tomorrow, Sid."

"Okay, Nolan . . . Nolan?"

"Yeah?"

"You mind if I ask you something else? Just one more thing, then I won't ask you any more questions."

Nolan shrugged.

"How much you made off the Boys so far?"

Nolan grinned the flat, humorless grin. "Don't know for sure. It's spread around, in banks. Maybe half a million. Maybe a little less."

Tisor laughed. "Shee-it! How long you gonna keep this up?"

Nolan stepped inside the cabin. He said, "You said one more question, Sid, and you've had it. Goodnight." He closed the door.

Tisor turned and headed for the Tempest. He got it started on the third try and wheeled out of the parking lot.

He knew damn well how long Nolan would play his little game with Charlie Franco.

Till one of them was dead.

4

When Tisor got out of bed the next morning and went downstairs to make coffee, he found Nolan waiting for him in the living room. Nolan was sitting on the couch, dressed in a yellow short-sleeved button-down shirt and brown slacks. He was smoking a cigarette and looking at the centerfold in Sid's latest *Playboy*, a photo of a nude girl smoking a cigar.

"Hi, Nolan." Tisor tried to conceal his surprise.

Nolan said, "Good morning," and tossed Tisor's *Playboy* down on the table. "Nice tits, but what can you do with a picture?"

Tisor said, "When you're my age, looking's sometimes all there is."

Nolan grunted.

"Want some coffee?"

"I started some when I got here. Ought to be done."

"I'll get it." Tisor trudged into the kitchen, the tile floor cold to his bare feet. He never ceased to be amazed by Nolan. He wanted to ask Nolan how he got in—Tisor had the night before locked the house up tight—but he knew Nolan had no patience with curiosity.

Nolan had risen at 6:30, after eight hours of sleep, and had taken a cab to Tisor's place. He'd sat down across the street on a bus stop bench to watch, hiding behind a newspaper. He saw that no one, outside of himself, was keeping an eye on

Tisor's house. And it didn't look like anybody besides Tisor was staying there, either. Sid looked clean, but over a single doubt Nolan would have frisked his own mother, had she been alive. Nolan sat staring at Sid's white two-story frame house, one of those boxes they churned out every hour on the hour in the fifties, and didn't get up from the bench till Sid's morning paper was delivered at 7:30. By 7:34 he had entered the house, through a basement window, and by 8:05 he'd searched every room, including the one Sid was sleeping in. Then, satisfied that Sid was clean, he had plopped down on the couch and started looking at the pictures in the November *Playboy*. At eight-thirty Sid came down in his green terry-cloth robe, looking like a corpse that had been goosed back to life.

Tisor brought Nolan a cup of coffee, black, and set a cup for himself on the table by Nolan. "Be back in a minute," Tisor said, and Nolan was on his second cup by the time Tisor came back down the stairs, dressed in a Hawaiian-print sport-shirt and baggy gray slacks. Tisor sat down in a chair across from Nolan and sipped his cup of coffee, which was too strong for him though he tried not to let on, since Nolan had made it. Nolan nearly let a grin out: he got a kick out of Tisor, who had been the most unlikely big-time "gangster" he had ever known.

Tisor was Charlie Franco's brother-in-law—his wife's maiden name was Rose Ann Franco—and had lived off Rosie's relatives since the day they were married. He had been fairly respectable before that, a CPA keeping books for several small firms and embezzling just a trifle; but his wife had insisted he take part in her brother's "business." It was quite painless for Tisor, who had switched to bookkeeper for the Family—he was an efficient, overpaid little wheel. And it was just like the world of business, all numbers in columns, and the closest he ever got to violence was the occasional Mickey Spillane novel he read.

He liked Nolan, who in spite of an apparent coldness seemed less an animal to Tisor than the rest of the gangsters playing businessman games. And in one of his rare moments of courage, Sid had taken a big chance hiding out Nolan when Nolan killed Tisor's no-good brother-in-law, that swishy bastard Sam Franco.

Now Tisor was all alone. He'd been alone for two years now, since he'd sent his little girl Irene off to college at Chelsey University. Before Irene was born, there had been Rosie, his wife; and when he lost Rosie, there was Diane, till she found somebody younger and richer. And always Irene, a wild but sweet kid, ever devoted to her old man. Tisor shook his head and sipped at the bitter coffee. Now there was nobody. Except Tisor himself, a lonely old man too afraid to take his own life.

Nolan said, "I have the same problem."

Tisor shook himself out of reverie. "What's that?"

"The past. I think about it, too. It's no good thinking about it."

Tisor smiled. That was the most personal remark Nolan had ever made to him.

Nolan poured himself another cup of the steaming black coffee and said, "What happened to Irene?"

Tisor's head lowered. "Suicide, they say."

"They don't know."

"Not for certain. You see . . . she was on LSD."

"Oh."

"She was on top of a building, fell off. The cops say she took a nose dive . . ."

"Yeah. Since she was tripping, they figure maybe she thought she could fly."

Tisor's eyes pleaded with Nolan. "Look into it for me, Nolan. Find out did she jump, did she fall, did she get pushed. But find out."

"What about the local law?"

"Hell," Tisor said. "The Chelsey cops couldn't find their dick in the dark."

"That where she went to school? Chelsey?"

"That's right, Nolan. Chelsey University at Chelsey, Illinois."

"Damn, Sid, I didn't want to come to Illinois for even a day, but here I am. Now you want me to hop over to Chelsey and play bloodhound for you."

"Listen to me, Nolan, hear it out . . ."

"Chelsey's only eighty miles from Chicago, Sid."

Tisor got guts for once. "Goddamn you, Nolan! Since when are you afraid of the Boys? Do you want to pay a debt you owe, or do you want to welsh on it?"

Nolan knew what Tisor said was the truth; he wasn't afraid of the Boys—he just had better things to do than make like a gumshoe. But it was a debt he owed, and it needed paying.

He said, "Go on, Sid. Tell me about it."

5

Tisor's eyes turned hard and he leaned toward Nolan. "My Irene was a wild one, Nolan. She could've taken that LSD trip on her own. And if so, maybe she did try a Superman off that building. But there were some things going on in Chelsey that might have got her killed."

"Like what?"

"She was home one weekend this summer and told me about this operation the Boys got going in Chelsey."

"What did she know about the Boys?"

"Well, before she went to college I broke it to her about my connection with them, explained it all. She took it pretty good, but it must've been a shock since I was always such a Puritan-type father. You know, not mean to her or anything, just old-fashioned."

"Yeah. Tell me what she saw going on in Chelsey." Nolan could see it would be a struggle getting the facts from Tisor; the guy would just keep reminiscing about the dead girl if Nolan let him.

"The Boys' operation, yeah. Well, they're selling everything from booze to pills to marijuana to LSD. All aimed at the college crowd."

"Irene a customer?"

"She never said, one way or another. I really can't imagine her taking drugs, but then, I'm her father, what do I know?

Anyway, she knew about the Boys' operation and their market. You see, there's this hippie colony in Chelsey she's got friends in. They number over five hundred and all live in the kind of slum section of town. It's got some publicity, maybe you read about it."

"I didn't. But Illinois seems too far east for a hippie colony."

"Why?"

Nolan lit a smoke. "Too cold. Communal living's swell, free love and all that. Till you freeze your ass off."

Tisor smiled, nodded. "You got a point. But these kids aren't what you'd call *real* hippies, if there is such a thing. Not California-style, anyway. They're rich kids, most of 'em, living off their parents' dough. They don't look so good in their beads and wilted flowers, and they don't smell so good, either. But they got money. Money for food, for heat . . ."

"For LSD," Nolan put in.

"And for LSD," Tisor agreed.

"Irene, was she one of the 'hippies'?"

"Borderline. She hung out with them, but she was putting seventy-five a month in an off-campus apartment she shared with a working girl named Vicki Trask. The Trask girl was laying out seventy-five a month, too."

"Hippies don't live in hundred-fifty buck apartments. Not 'real' ones."

"Well, Irene and her roommate weren't deep-dyed Chelsey hippies. But, like I said, even the most sincere ones are just leeches sucking money off their parents. Chelsey is a rich-kid school, you know."

"You think the Boys got a good thing going for them, then? Got any ideas what they're getting for one trip?"

An LSD trip took 100 micrograms of d-lysergic acid diethylamide tartrate and cost pennies to make. "I think they're getting around eight or ten bucks a trip," said Tisor.

Nolan scratched his as yet unshaven chin. "They're not making much off that. Granted, there isn't much money wrapped up in producing LSD. Any two-bit chemist with the materials and a vacuum pump can whip up a batch. But even a confirmed tripper only takes a trip or two a week."

"It's a big campus, Nolan. Almost ten thousand students."

"Still, you can't figure more than four hundred trips a week. That's less than four grand coming in."

"That isn't so bad, Nolan."

"Yeah, but that's their big seller, isn't it, LSD?"

"They're selling booze, too, to the frat crowd. Most any kid on campus might use pep pills now and then. Big market for pot."

"They selling any hard stuff?"

"Heroin, you mean?"

"Yeah."

"Hell, no. Nolan. The Commission of families in New York's got control over stuff like that. You know that. Anybody caught with a dope set-up is going to get their ass kicked hard unless the Commission's okayed it."

Nolan shook his head. "I don't understand this. LSD. Nickels and dimes. Why are the Boys fooling around with it?"

"Nolan, they got other things going for 'em in Chelsey! They got gambling, they got a massage parlor, a strip joint or two . . ."

"Don't bull me, Sid. Take the college out of Chelsey and there's only seven thousand people left. The Family doesn't mess with small-time operations unless there's a reason. I know they can't be pulling in even five thousand a week, before expenses."

"Nolan, I . . ."

"You're not telling the whole story, Sid."

Tisor looked at the floor. He didn't want to meet Nolan's eyes, if he could help it. "George Franco's running the Chelsey operation."

Nolan's laugh was short, harsh. No wonder the set-up was small-time! An LSD ring, what a joke. You could save all the money you'd make off a racket like that and go to Riverview Park once a year.

"Sid," Nolan said, "you and I both know what George Franco is."

George Franco was the younger brother of Charlie Franco and the late Sam Franco, and also of Tisor's late wife, Rosie. George: the obese, incompetent younger brother who couldn't cut it and got sent places where he wouldn't cause trouble. A glutton, a coward, and simple-minded to boot.

"Okay," Sid admitted, "it's no big set-up. It's a small operation that Charlie gave George to give him something to do."

Nolan got up from the couch. "Be seeing you, Sid."

"Wait, Nolan, will you wait just a minute!"

"Having George Franco on hand makes this too close to home where the Boys are concerned, and at the same time makes any possible score small potatoes. Be seeing you."

"Listen to me, will you just listen? It's better than you think. George doesn't have full charge, he's more or less a figurehead. There's a financial secretary, of sorts, who really runs the show. I don't know the guy's name, but he's no dummy."

"Where do you get your information?"

"George is my brother-in-law, remember?"

"Does he know Irene's related?"

"He might have met her when she was a kid, but he

doesn't know I have . . . *had* a girl who went to Chelsey. At least as far as I know he doesn't. That dumb asshole doesn't know much of anything."

"I'll grant you that, Sid."

"Look, George talked to me on the phone last week, social call, you know? I pumped him a little. They're pulling in at least six grand a week."

"Sid, it's my life you're trading bubblegum cards against."

"Don't forget you owe me, Nolan, remember that! And there's going to be close to forty thousand in it for you, I swear."

"At six grand a week, how do you figure? The Boys send in a bagman every Wednesday and take the last week's earnings back to Chicago. That's s.o.p. with the Family. I know these set-ups, Sid."

"But they don't come in weekly! Chelsey is so close to Chicago they don't bother sending a man every week."

"How often *do* they pick it up?"

"Every six weeks. But I don't know where they keep it till then."

"How about the local bank?"

"Nope, I checked it. They must keep it on ice somewhere."

"So there ought to be around forty thousand in this for me, Sid, that right?"

"I think so, Nolan. Maybe more."

Nolan thought for a moment. Then: "What makes you think this operation in Chelsey has anything to do with your daughter's death?"

"Damn it, Nolan, I figure if they didn't do anything outside of sell that cube of LSD she's supposed to have swallowed, then they killed her, didn't they? Besides, because she was my kid she knew things about the Boys and the connection they had to Chelsey. If she let any of that slip to the wrong person, it could have got her killed. And . . ." Tisor's eyes were filmed over and he looked down at his hands, folded tightly in his lap.

"And what?"

"Nolan, I have to know *why* she died. I have to know."

"It's enough she's dead, Sid."

"*No, it isn't!* She was the only thing I had to show for my entire life, she was the only thing I had left to care about! I'm not like you, Nolan . . . I can't let go of something that important with a shrug."

There were a few moments of silence, while Tisor regained a modicum of control. Nolan sat and seemed to be studying the thin ropes of smoke coiling off his cigarette.

"If I find out Irene was murdered," Nolan said, his voice a low, soft monotone, "and I find the one who did it, what am I supposed to do?"

"That's up to you, Nolan."

"You expect me to kill somebody?"

"I know you, Nolan. I expect if anyone needs killing, you'll take care of it."

"I'm not making any promises, you understand."

"I understand, Nolan."

"All right, then. Get some paper and write down every speck of information you got on Irene and Chelsey. The college, her friends, the Boys' operation, George, everything you know about it. And put in a recent snap of Irene."

"Right." Tisor got a notebook and a pen and Nolan smoked two cigarettes while Tisor filled up three pages for him. Tisor gave Nolan the notebook, then went to a drawer to find a picture of his daughter.

"Here she is," he said, holding a smudged Polaroid shot.

"That's old, Sid—nothing newer? This is what she

looked like when I knew her."

"She got prettier in the last couple years since you saw her. I had her nose fixed, did you know that?"

"No." She'd been a dark-haired girl, beautiful but for a nose that could have opened bottles, and it was nice that Sid had got it bobbed for her, but Nolan hardly saw it worth talking about when she was dead.

Tisor's eyes were cloudy. "They . . . they told me on the phone that . . . she . . . she fell ten stories . . . it was awful. They sent her body back on a train for the . . . funeral. I had to have them keep the casket closed . . ."

"Don't waste your tears on the dead, Sid," Nolan told him. "You got to mourn somebody, mourn the living—they got it tougher."

"You . . . you don't understand how it is . . ."

Hell, Nolan thought, dust doesn't give a damn. But he said, "Sure, Sid, sure."

"Let me tell you about her, Nolan . . ."

"I got to be going now, Sid."

"Yeah . . . yeah, that's right. I can't tell you how much I . . . I appreciate this . . . Nolan, thanks."

"Sure." He headed for the door. "See you around."

"Yeah . . . uh . . . so long, Nolan . . . you going by bus?"

Nolan looked at him and said, "You ask too many questions, Sid," and closed the door.

Tisor watched through the picture window and saw Nolan board a city bus routed for downtown Peoria.

There Nolan found a Hertz office and rented a midnight-blue Lincoln in Tisor's name. He drove it back to his motel, packed and cleaned up, then checked out.

He could make Chelsey by noon if he kicked it.

6

George Franco was a satisfied man.

He was not happy, but there was satisfaction, a certain contentment in his life.

He realized this as he lay on the soft double bed in his penthouse apartment, watching his woman get dressed. She was a leggy whore, with good firm breasts, and she was taking her time about fastening the garter snaps as she replaced her black hose. Her tousled black hair fell to her shoulders, and her once-pretty face wore a tight red line for a mouth. George liked the look of her hard, well-built body, but he didn't like her equally hard face which spoke of something other than love.

But she was his woman, hired or not, and he was lucky to have her and knew it. Especially when you were a repulsive glob of fat, as George resignedly recognized himself to be.

She was dressed now, as dressed as possible considering the black sheath hit mid-thigh. She did her imitation of a smile for him and said, "Tomorrow, same time, Georgie?"

"Yeah, Francie. Tomorrow. Sure was good today."

The whore smiled some more and said, "Yeah, sure was," because that was her job. Her fingers rippled a little wave at her employer and she left.

George sat up on the bed, poured the last shot out of the bottle of Scotch he and the woman had emptied during the day—the courthouse clock across the way was bonging four—and he drank it down. He held his liquor well, he knew he did; it was the one thing he could do well. Then he settled back with a good cigar and thought about his life.

Satisfied, content. Not happy, but you can't have everything.

After all, he had fifty cent cigars when he wanted them, and a fifty dollar woman when he wanted her. He lived in a five hundred buck a month secret penthouse (over a drugstore) with five rooms and two color T.V.'s and two cans and two big double beds and three bars and lots of soft red carpet. His bars were well-stocked with all the liquor he could possibly drink; and he had all the food he could eat, as prepared by his personal chef, who came in twice a day. The chef lived down the street in an apartment shared with George's maid.

There were disadvantages, George realized that. People still didn't like him. They never had, they never would. It was a kind of reverse magnetism he possessed. His woman, for example. You can only buy a woman from the neck down, he told himself over and over again, but you can never buy the head, except for the mouth of course. And his men, the ones who were supposed to protect him, they didn't like him. And his chef didn't like him—the chef could *stand* George, and seemed to *kind of* like him, but that was only because George was a good eater and, as such, a pleasure to cook for.

Hell, he thought, not even his brothers had liked him.

Not to mention his father.

But Momma (*requiescat in pace*) had liked him.

The best move he had ever made was being born of that sweet woman. Being born of the woman had made him the son of Carlo Franco (*requiescat in pace*), a big man in Chicago "business." And the brother of Charlie Franco and Rosie

Franco (*requiescat in pace*) and Sam Franco (*requiescat in pace*), who didn't like him but provided for him. Especially after Poppa died and Charlie and Sam took the reins of the "business."

Charlie and Sam looked out for their younger brother very well, in spite of their lack of brotherly love for him. Back in '58 they had put him on the board of directors of the business—made him one of "The Boys." But when George fumbled away over a half million dollars in his treasurer capacity, in a virtuoso display of incompetence, he was replaced by Lou Goldstein.

George cursed Goldstein as regularly as he ate. That goddamn Jew! What would Poppa (*requiescat in pace*) think about a Jew being one of the Family, for Christ's sake!

But even George knew that Goldstein could keep good books. And Goldstein was a veteran of the "business" with a talent for seeing to it that other people kept good books. George, on the other hand, had trouble carrying a number over to the tens column.

George rose from the bed and headed for the bar a few steps away; he needed a fresh bottle of Scotch. Another disadvantage of wealth, George decided, was it made you waddle when you walked. Especially when you tipped the scales, as George did, at an even two hundred and eighty. When he walked on the plush red carpet, he left tracks that took their time raising into place again.

As he stood at the bar pouring a shot of Scotch, he heard a knock at the door. He glanced at his watch and said, "It's open, Elliot," and downed the Scotch. Time for Elliot.

A man entered the room, a man as thin as George was heavy. He wore a powder blue suit, tailored, with a blue-striped tie. His face was bony and pockmarked, and his large black horn-rimmed glasses made his head seem small. Behind the lenses of the glasses were watery blue eyes. His teeth were very white.

"How are things going for us, Elliot?"

Elliot was George's financial secretary—the strong prime minister to George's weak queen. Elliot said, "Things are fine, Mr. Franco."

George poured another shot, said, "You want anything?"

"Ginger ale would be fine."

George poured a glass, dropped a few ice cubes into it and left it on the bar for Elliot to retrieve. He headed for the bed, where he sat among the unmade sheets, wondering why Elliot never drank hard stuff, wondering why he never smoked, or never seemed to have any interest in women. Maybe he was queer, who could tell about the guy?

Elliot went after the ginger ale, then found a chair.

George, sitting on the bed, said, "How's the college kid trade? They still buyin' what we're sellin'?"

"Business is good, Mr. Franco."

"How about the feds? You said last time there was a rumor about feds."

There had been a rumble that federal men were going to look into the Chelsey situation because of some unfavorable publicity concerning local college kids and LSD. There had been a girl who had jumped from a building while on a trip. There had been four trippers, it had been reported, who were in the hospital after having eaten magic sugar cubes and then deciding to stare at the sun. A day of sun-gazing, supposedly, resulted in all four going blind.

"It's still just a rumor about the feds," Elliot said. "Nobody paid much attention to the girl who went off the building, and the story about the sun-gazers going blind turned out to be a fake. Just one of those stories that got started."

"That's good to hear," George said. "No trouble about the girl who fell off the building?"

"No, it's blown over. Phil got the thing played down."

Phil Saunders was Elliot's cousin; he was also the police chief in Chelsey.

"What was that girl's name?"

"Tisor," Elliot said. "I think that's it. Tisor."

"Coincidence," George said, gulping his Scotch. "My sister married a guy named Tisor. Used to work under Goldstein."

"Is that so." Elliot was tapping his foot, not nervous, just anxious to bid George good-bye. At least that was the way George interpreted it.

George leaned back on the bed and waved his arms with a flourish. "You're doin' a good job, Elliot, and I'm gonna put in the word for you with my brother Charlie."

Elliot's smug smile stung George. *Skinny little shit! Smirking little bastard! I'm George Franco, and you're nobody!*

"Just keep up the good work," George continued, murdering Elliot over and over again in his mind.

"I have your allowance, Mr. Franco."

That damn condescending tone!

"Leave it on the bar, Elliot."

Elliot nodded, got up from the chair and laid down his empty glass and an envelope on the bar. The envelope contained two-hundred dollars, George's allowance for the next week. There were bank accounts George could draw upon, and his expenses were taken care of by Elliot on Charlie Franco's orders; but to simplify things for George, this spending money was allotted him. Pin money.

"See you, Mr. Franco."

"Good-bye, Elliot."

Elliot left silently.

George stared at the ceiling and pounded a fist into the soft bed. Then he sighed and rolled over on his stomach.

Yes, it was a good life for him. His only real job was to keep out of Elliot's way. It was perfectly all right for him to pretend that he was Elliot's superior, Elliot went along with it pretty good, but his direct orders from brother Charlie were to stay the hell out of Elliot's operation.

Kissing ass didn't bother him *too* much. Not when it stayed relatively painless, like this.

Not when he was safe, content.

After all, wasn't he the smart one? Hadn't his brother Sam (*requiescat in pace*) got himself all shot to hell by that crazy animal named Nolan? Wasn't Charlie scared crapless all the time for fear death'll strike him down like Sam, either through this Nolan clown or some other maniac connected to the family "business"?

George chuckled. *He* was the smart Franco. He stayed away from trouble in a little town in Illinois, getting fat on fine foods, getting drunk on good booze and screwing nice-looking broads. He got nowhere near the fireworks, yet he got all the benefits.

Look at poor Sam (*requiescat in pace*). Shot down like a common criminal! And to think that psychopath Nolan was still running around loose, gunning for brother Charlie.

"No sir," George said aloud, "none of that crap for me."

"None of what crap for you, George?"

George rolled over and looked up. He hadn't seen the man enter, he hadn't heard him either. He was a tall, mustached man, his brown hair graying at the temples, dressed in a tailored tan suit and holding a .38 Smith and Wesson in his hand.

"Who . . . who the hell're you? You work for me? I never seen you before."

"Think. You've seen my picture."

"I . . . I don't know you."

The man sat on the edge of the bed, prodded George with the .38. "My name's Nolan."

TWO

1

Nolan arrived in Chelsey, Illinois, a few minutes past noon. He let a Holiday Inn go by, and a Howard Johnson's, then picked a non-chain motel called the Travel Nest. It was a pleasant-looking yellow building, an L-shaped two stories; its sign promised an indoor heated pool, color television and a vacancy. Nolan pulled into the car port outside the motel office and went in.

"Yes sir?" The manager, a middle-aged man with dark, slightly thinning hair, gave Nolan a professional smile.

Nolan said he'd need a room for a week, filled out the registration, using the name Earl Webb. He listed his occupation as journalist and his hometown as Philadelphia. The manager asked if he wished to pay the $65 room rate when he checked out or . . .

Nolan gave the man two fifties. "Make it a nice room."

"Yes, sir!" The manager eyed the registration. "Are you a newspaperman, Mr. Webb?"

"No," Nolan said. "I'm with a new magazine out of Philadelphia. Planning a big first issue. It's going to be on the order of *Look*, except monthly."

"Really?" The manager's eyes went round with interest. Nolan smiled inwardly; he hoped everybody would bite his line as eagerly as this guy did.

"Come with me, Mr. Webb," the manager said. He turned

to a younger copy of himself, most likely his son or kid brother, and snapped, "Take over, Jerome."

Jerome took over and the manager followed Nolan back outside to the Lincoln.

"We can park your car, if you like."

"I'll park it."

The manager told Nolan where the room was and turned and walked briskly toward the far end of the yellow building. Nolan got into the Lincoln and drove it into the empty space near the door the manager was entering. He liked the looks of the motel, well kept-up, with separate balconies for each room on the upper story, private sun porches for the lower. He got out of the Lincoln, took his suitcase and clothes-bags from the trunk, then locked the car.

He met the manager at the head of the stairs and followed him to room 17. It was large, smelled fresh and was mostly a pastel green. The spread on the double bed was a darker green and the French doors leading out to the balcony were ivory-white. Nolan looked in at the bath and shower, found it clean and walked out on the balcony, which afforded him a view of the wooded area to the rear of the motel. There was a color TV. Nolan said it would do.

"If you need anything else, just call down to the office and ask for me—Mr. Barnes. Oh, and there's a steak house across the street. And the pool is just down the hall."

"If you're fishing for a tip, I already slipped you an extra thirty-five."

The little man looked hurt, but he didn't say anything; he just forced a weak smile and started to leave. Nolan immediately regretted falling out of character. He had to make himself be decent to people, even insignificant ones.

"Hey," Nolan called softly.

The manager, halfway down the hall by now, turned

and said, "Yes, Mr. Webb?"

"Com'ere, Mr. Barnes."

Nolan reached into his front shirt pocket and pulled out a pack of cigarettes. He offered one to Barnes, who accepted it. He lit one himself, smiled his tight smile at Barnes in a semblance of good will.

"Mr. Barnes, the assignment I'm on for my magazine is important to me. A big opportunity. I could use your help."

Barnes grinned like a chimp. "I'll be happy to assist you, Mr. Webb."

"I wonder if maybe there's somewhere in town reporters might hang out."

"Well . . . several bars come to mind. There's a fairly good restaurant where the *Globe* guys go to talk. Called the Big Seven."

"Where is it?"

"It's down the hill from the football stadium, by Front Street bridge."

"Big Seven, huh?"

"Yes, it's a sports type hangout. The Chelsey U football team is in the Big Seven conference, you know."

"Any place else?"

"Some bars downtown. Dillon's, maybe, or Eastgate Tavern. What you going to write on, the hippies?"

"Maybe."

"Well, Hal Davis did a big write-up on the anti-draft demonstration last week. Hippies, yippies, the whole SDS crew. A bunch of 'em slaughtered a live calf on the steps of the student union, then tossed it at some Dow Chemical people who came down to C.U. to interview seniors for jobs."

"Interesting. He didn't happen to do a write-up on that girl who fell off the building a while back?"

"Don't know, Mr. Webb. There *was* a write-up on that,

but I can't remember any details. Say, I'm saving my old *Globe*s for a paper drive one of my kids is on. If you want to look at some of 'em, I could bring up a batch."

"Fine. Bring them up for the past couple months and you got another ten bucks."

Barnes smiled. "Don't bother, Mr. Evans. Glad to help, you being a real writer and all." Then he trotted off after the papers.

Good, thought Nolan. This way he wouldn't have to go down to the newspaper and ask to see back files. It wouldn't pay to show his face claiming to be a writer when he didn't have enough knowledge or a solid enough cover to fake it around pros.

He eased out of the tan suitcoat, hung it over a chair and started to unpack, leaving most of his things, including a spare .38 Colt and several boxes of ammunition, in the suitcase. He hung his clothes-bags in the closet and thought about taking a shower, but then decided against it. He was too tired for that, so he flopped down on the bed and closed his eyes. He yawned, stretched his arms behind him, brushing against the phone book on the nightstand in back of him. He pulled the book down from the stand and looked up the *Globe*'s number.

When he got the newsroom Nolan asked to speak to Mr. Davis. Mr. Davis was not in, was there a message? No message, he could call Mr. Davis later.

There was a knock and it was Barnes with the papers. Nolan thanked him and took the stack from him and laid it on the bed.

He leafed through the papers till he came to one published the day after Irene's death. The notes Tisor had given him were fairly complete, but any extra information might help. Besides, Tisor hadn't even come to Chelsey to pick up the body; Irene Tisor's body had journeyed home by train.

There were three articles on the death, one published the evening after she died, one the next evening and one the evening after that. The article printed the evening after her death wryly commented that "certain factions in Chelsey have made LSD, among other items, easily accessible to C.U. students." The by-line read Hal Davis. The other two articles, under the same by-line, played down the incident, largely ignoring the LSD and its implications and labeling the death "apparent suicide."

A white-wash job.

And Nolan could guess who was holding the brush.

The Chelsey arm of Franco-Goldstein enterprises was trying to slip the LSD part of the story under a rock to keep federal men out. This meant, one way or another, the Family branch in Chelsey had gotten to Hal Davis.

Nolan lit another cigarette and remembered George Franco.

Would it be stupid to reveal himself to a Franco?

Nolan had never met George and had only seen him once, at a cocktail party some years ago at Sam Franco's. Nolan knew George by reputation, though, and from what he'd heard about the younger Franco, it should take only a few screws put to him to make him tell his life story. George had made a name for himself as a coward, and not a smart coward at that. Some meaningful threats might both pry information from George and keep his mouth shut about Nolan's presence in Chelsey.

Nolan tried the *Globe* again, couldn't get Davis, then got up from bed and, phone book under his arm, left the room, grabbing his tan suitcoat from the chair. He went out to the Lincoln, climbed in and roared toward Chelsey.

As he drove through the shaded residential streets, Nolan

felt Chelsey was more a postcard than a city. He had heard there was a slum in Chelsey, but that he would have to see to believe.

In seven minutes he reached the downtown area. It was a typical small-town business district, built around a square, with all the businesses enclosing a quaint crumbling courthouse which stood in the center collecting dust. There were people bundled warmly against the cold Illinois wind, rushing up and down the sidewalks, visibly pained to move that quickly. Birds and bird-dung clung to the courthouse and Nolan wondered why the hell they didn't fly south or something. At first Nolan didn't see any old men in front of the courthouse, as he expected there to be, but after he parked his car and walked half-way around the square, he saw them at last. They were sitting in the shade of a large leafy tree, bench-bound, tobacco-mouthed, as motionless as the twin Civil War cannons in front of them.

He checked Dillon's Tap, found it empty except for a blowsy redhead talking to the bartender. No Davis, no other reporters to ask about Davis.

He didn't find Davis or colleagues in the Eastgate Tavern, where two on-duty policemen were drinking beer. He didn't want to talk to them.

Nolan went back to his rented Lincoln and headed toward the Chelsey University campus, which lay beyond the downtown district. The downtown continued on three streets north of the square, made up primarily of collegiate shops and bookstores; then the campus lay just after that, on a bluff overlooking the Chelsey River.

The river was little more than a wide stream, with several footbridges and four traffic bridges crossing it. The rest of Chelsey and the C.U. campus, football stadium included, were on the other side of the river. Nolan drove over the

Front Street bridge and saw a large unlit neon saying Big 7. He pulled into the parking lot and went in.

The place was dark and smoke hung over it like a gray cloud. Nolan couldn't tell whether or not, as the motel manager had said, it was a fairly nice restaurant, simply because he couldn't see it very well. All he could see clearly were football action shots trying in vain to break the monotony of the room's pine-paneled walls. Then he spotted two men in wrinkled suits, one blue and one grey, standing at the bar arguing over a long dead play out of a long dead Rose Bowl game.

"Excuse me," Nolan said.

The two guys stopped mid-play and gave Nolan twin what-the-hell-do-you-want sneers.

Nolan said, "Where can I find Hal Davis?"

The two guys looked at each other in acknowledgment of Nolan being a stranger to both of them. Then one of the guys, a chunky ex-high school tackle perhaps, said, "Maybe Hal Davis likes privacy. Maybe he don't care to be found."

"If you know where he is, I'd appreciate it you tell me."

The guy looked at Nolan, looked at Nolan's eyes.

"He's over at the corner table. Facin' the wall."

Nolan nodded.

The two men returned to the play and Nolan headed for the corner table, where a sandy-haired man of around fifty sat nursing a glass of bourbon.

"Mr. Davis?"

He glanced up. His eyes were blood-shot and heavily bagged and the hands around the glass were shaky. He wasn't drunk, but he wished he was. His lips barely moved as he said, "I don't know you, mister."

"My name's Webb. Care if I sit?"

"I don't care period."

Nolan sat. He looked at Davis, caught the man's eyes and

held them. "You look like a man who got pushed and didn't like it."

Davis shook Nolan's gaze and stared into his glass of bourbon. "I said I don't know you, Webb. I think maybe I don't want to know you."

Nolan shrugged. "I'm telling people I'm a magazine writer, Mr. Davis. But that's not who I am or why I came to Chelsey."

"Why, then? You come to drop out and turn on?"

"I'm a private investigator," Nolan told him. "From Philadelphia. I been hired by a client . . . who'll remain nameless of course . . . to contact a Mr. George Franco."

Davis said, "You know something, Webb? You don't look like a private investigator to me. You look like a hood. You got something under your left armpit besides hair, your fancy suit isn't cut so well that I can't tell that. What's it you're after in Chelsey? You got a contract on Franco?"

"No. What if I did?"

"I wouldn't give a damn."

"You getting shoved around by the Boys, Mr. Davis?"

"The boys? What boys are those?"

So, Nolan thought, maybe Davis doesn't know about the Chelsey hook-up with the Chicago outfit; maybe he's just a small-town newsman getting pressured by "local hoods."

Nolan said, "Let me put it this way . . . are George Franco and his associates telling you what to say in the *Globe*?"

"You mean what *not* to say, don't you? Sure, they're tellin' me, and they got some pretty goddamn persuasive ways of telling, too."

"I want Franco's address."

Davis downed the dregs of the bourbon. He smiled; one of his front teeth was chipped in half. "I'll get it capped one of these days," he said, gesturing to it with the emptied shot glass. "For a while I'm leavin' it like this, so I can look in the mirror when I get up mornings and think about what a chicken-shit I am."

Nolan said, "Franco's address."

Davis shook his head. "It's not an address. It doesn't exist, not officially, anyway. It's a fancy penthouse deal, only it's above a drug store. Berry Drug, right down on the square, across from the courthouse and cannons. There's a fire escape in back that'll lead you to a bedroom window."

"Any bars on it?"

"Nope. Just a regular glass window. They don't bother protecting fat George *that* much. Thinks his place is a real secret."

"Is it?"

"It was." He grinned his air-conditioned grin. "But it looks like the secret's out, doesn't it?"

Nolan dropped a twenty on the table and left.

He drove back across the bridge and parked his car several blocks away from Berry Drug. He went into a hardware store and bought a glass-cutter, then walked to the courthouse lawn. He sat on one of the benches by an old man who smelled like a urinal and watched the drug store for about an hour. A black-haired whore in a short black shift came out, then a thin man in a powder-blue suit went in and came back out in less than ten minutes.

After a while Nolan strolled around behind the drug store and climbed the fire escape and used the glass-cutter on the window. It was broad daylight, but the 'scape was at an angle and Nolan figured a daytime attack would be less expected.

He slipped into the plush red-carpeted flat, and crept over to the bed, where an extremely fat man in a silk dressing gown lay on his stomach, half-asleep and talking to himself.

Nolan got out his .38 and, after a brief exchange of conversation, introduced himself to George Franco.

"My name's Nolan."

It was four fifteen p.m.

Back in Peoria Sid Tisor was wondering if Nolan had reached Chelsey yet.

2

Nolan strolled over to the bar, laid his gun on the counter and helped himself to a shot of Jim Beam. He glanced over at George, who was sitting on the edge of the bed, his plump fists clenching the bedspread. George's forehead was beaded with sweat; his mouth hung loosely above two double chins.

Nolan asked George if he wanted a drink.

George tried to answer yes but couldn't spit it out.

Nolan, seeing an open bottle of Haig and Haig on the counter, poured a healthy glass of Scotch and dropped in an ice cube. He retrieved his .38 from the counter and took the glass of Scotch to George, who grabbed for it and began sloshing it down.

Nolan dragged a chair to the bed and sat.

"Let's talk, George."

"You must be out of your mind!"

"You're not the first to suggest that."

"What are you doing here? What do you want?"

Nolan shrugged. "I just want to 'rap.' "

"When my brother Charlie finds out about you bein' in Chelsey . . ."

Nolan lifted the .38 and let him look down the long barrel. "Your brother isn't going to find out, George. And neither are any of your associates."

George's eyes golf-balled. "You . . . you think you can threaten me? *Me?* I'm a Franco!"

Nolan, his mouth a grim line, said, "So was Sam."

George Franco looked into the flint grey eyes of the man who had murdered Sam Franco. He swallowed hard.

Nolan lowered the .38. "I won't hurt you unless I have to. I got a hunch this deal doesn't have a lot to do with you."

"What are you talking about?"

Nolan finished the whiskey, went back and poured another. "I'm here to look into a matter. The matter may concern the Chelsey operation you're involved in. And it may not."

George was trembling, like a huge bowl of fleshy gelatin. "What . . . what do you want from me?"

"Information."

"What kind?"

"Different kinds. Let's start with a name. Irene Tisor. What does that name mean to you?"

"A girl, that's all."

"What about her?"

"She fell off a building."

"Is that all you know about her?"

"She was on LSD."

"Did she fall?"

"I don't know."

"You said she fell."

"She could have."

"Was she pushed?"

"I don't know."

"What connection does your operation have with her death?"

"She got the LSD from one of our sellers, I suppose. So we put on some pressure to cover it up. We didn't want feds coming in and bothering us."

"What kind of pressure, George?"

"I don't know."

"Had you ever heard the name Irene Tisor before?"

"No . . . I got a brother-in-law named Tisor. You probably knew him from Chicago. Sid Tisor?"

"I heard the name before," Nolan said.

"You don't suppose Irene Tisor was a relative? His kid or something?"

"You tell me."

"Naw, I don't think so. Back in the old days, Sid was nicer to me than a lot of people; we keep in touch. Just last week we talked on the phone and he didn't say a word about any relative of his being killed in Chelsey."

Nolan grunted noncommittally. Well, looked like George didn't connect Irene to Sid. But then how much did George really know about the operation?

"What kind of money you getting for one hit of LSD?"

George said, "I don't know."

"You selling pot?"

"Sure."

"How much is a lid going for?"

"I don't know."

"You selling heroin?"

"I don't know."

"What percent of your income's from selling alcohol to underage buyers?"

"I don't know."

"How about barbiturates? Amphetamines?"

"I don't know."

Nolan rose, balled his fist and resisted the urge to splatter fat George all over the fancy apartment. He holstered the .38 and got out his cigarettes. Lighting one, he said, "You don't have a goddamn thing to do with the operation, do you, George?"

George's face flushed. "I do *so!* I . . . I . . ."

"You what?"

"I supervise! I do a lot of things . . . I . . ."

Nolan ignored him. "Who's the boss?"

George didn't say anything.

"Somebody's got to run the show. Who is it?"

George remained silent.

Nolan took out the gun again, disgustedly. "Who, George?"

George's face turned blue.

"I'm going to have to get nasty, now, George."

"It's Elliot!" he sputtered. "Elliot, Elliot."

"Elliot. He's your . . . secretary?" Nolan searched his mind for the expression Tisor had used in describing the position.

"Yes, my financial secretary."

"What's his full name?"

"Irwin Taylor Elliot."

"Where's he live?"

"In town, on Fairport Drive. It's a fancy residential district. High rent."

"What's his address?"

"I don't know . . . but it's in the phone book."

"He's got a listed number?"

"He's got a real estate agency that fronts him."

"Is there anybody else with power in town?"

"Just Elliot's cousin—the police chief."

"That's handy. What's his name?"

"Saunders. Phil Saunders."

Nolan drew on the cigarette, blew out a cloud of smoke. "If you're holding out any information, George, it's best you tell me now."

George shook his head no. "I don't know nothing else."

"You're a good boy, George." Nolan walked around the room for a few minutes, playing mental ping-pong. Then he said, "How do you get in this place . . . besides up the fire escape?"

"Through a door next to the can downstairs, in the drug store."

"Fitting. Any of your men down there?"

"During store hours there's always either a clerk or an assistant pharmacist on duty downstairs to watch out for me." George's face twisted bitterly for a moment. "Sure do a hell of a job protecting me, don't they?"

"Swell," Nolan agreed. "You got a phone here?"

"Yeah."

"What's the number?"

"CH7-2037. Why?"

"Is it bugged?"

"I don't think so. Why would they bother checking up on *me?*"

"You got a point." Nolan repeated the number to himself silently. "You'll be hearing from me now and then, George."

George looked pleadingly at Nolan. "Look, I don't know anything. You aren't gonna get any good out of hurting me. You . . . you aren't gonna . . . do anything to me . . . are you?"

Nolan hunted for an ash tray, found one, stabbed out his cigarette. "I won't touch you, George, unless you cross me. But finger me and you're dead."

"Oh, I wouldn't . . ."

"I should put a bullet in your head right now, when I think of it. You're a bad risk."

"Oh, no, you can't . . ."

"I can, and I have. I killed six men in the past eight years. Not to mention the ones I left wounded."

"I never did anything to you, Nolan . . ."

"Don't sic anybody on me and we'll get along fine. But you tell your brother about me, or that Elliot, or anyone else, and you'll die wishing you hadn't."

"Nolan, I wouldn't . . ."

"Shut up. You don't think I'm working alone, do you?"

"What?"

"I got three men watching you," Nolan lied. "They'll kill you the moment anybody puts a hand on me. So getting rid of me would only assure you of dying."

George lay back on the bed and moaned. He looked like a beached whale, only whales didn't sweat.

Nolan finished his whiskey and headed for the window.

3

The national anthem woke Nolan and he sat up on the bed and checked his watch. Quarter after twelve. He had returned to the Travel Nest after eating at the steak house across the way and watched television until it put him to sleep. Now he felt wide awake; and his shoulders, his back, felt tense.

He got out of the now-wrinkled tan suit and put on his black swim trunks. He grabbed up a pack of cigarettes and matches, draped a towel over his shoulders and headed down the hall.

The door leading into the pool was closed but not locked. A sign hung on it reading "Life Guard on Duty 9 a.m. to 9 p.m. The management cannot be responsible for after-hour swimmers. Swim only at your own risk. T. C. Barnes, Manager."

It was a small pool, filling most of a small room. From the door to the pool was an area where people could stretch out beach towels and dump their belongings while swimming. Other than that initial area beyond the entrance, there was a scant three feet around the pool's edge bordering it. Paintings of sea horses rode the blue walls, and the air hung thick with heat and chlorine.

He dove in the deep end and swam several laps and turned over on his back for a while; then he climbed out and dove off the little diving board at the far end of the pool.

Swimming on his back again, Nolan relaxed and enjoyed the warmth of the pool, the all-encompassing feeling of the water around him. Even in a thimble like this, Nolan got a sensation of freedom when swimming. It gave him room to reach out.

Several minutes later Nolan heard the door open. Another late swimmer, a young lady perhaps? That'd be nice, Nolan thought, floating on his back. Then his fantasy was over before it began when his ears reported heavy, plodding footsteps splashing in the dampness of the room.

"Everybody out of the pool," a harsh voice grated. Nolan swam to one side, set his hands in the gutters and pushed himself out. He stood and looked at the intruders.

Two men, obviously local color. A Mutt and Jeff combination.

The short one, a pale, bloodless-looking specimen, owned the low voice. He wore a pink shirt with red pin-stripes, with a thin black tie loosened around the collar, and a gold sportcoat. His brown slacks were uncuffed and ended a little high over his white socks and brown shoes.

His companion was a tall and beefy dope who wore a grey business suit a size too small. His eyes were expressionless brown marbles under a sloping forehead; his features were hard and battered, his cheeks acned. His mouth, though, was surprisingly delicate, almost feminine.

The short one said, "Mr. Webb? You *are* Mr. Webb, I assume?" He had dark plastered-down hair with motorcycle sideburns to contrast his chalky complexion. A hick trying to look hip.

"I'm Webb. What do you want?"

The big ox nudged his partner's shoulder and smirked. The smaller man, who seemed to think himself intelligent, smiled sneeringly at Nolan.

"Care to let me in on the joke?"

"You *are* the joke, Mr. Webb," the short one said, then he and ox shared a round of laughter.

Nolan remained calm. This was a situation he could handle, but he was pissed with himself for allowing it to happen. Amateurs, damn it, he'd let amateurs catch up with him. And the maddening thing was he too had acted like an amateur, by coming unarmed for his impromptu late-night swim.

"Allow me to make an introduction," the side-burned spokesman said. "I'm Dinneck. And my partner here is Tulip."

"A rose by any other name," Nolan said.

"Is he making fun of me, Dinneck?"

"Tulip, keep quiet, okay?"

"Okay."

Dinneck smiled again, the smile of a guy who sells watches on a corner. He said, "Mr. Webb, we don't want any trouble from you. All we want is answers."

Nolan said, "Who sent you? George Franco?"

Dinneck nodded to Tulip, who removed his coat. Tulip's chest was massive and his short-sleeved white shirt was banded by a leather strap which supported a shoulder holster cradling a .45. Tulip folded his muscular arms like a guard protecting a Sultan's harem. There was an innocent smile planted on his bud of a mouth.

Dinneck said, "From now on, Mr. Webb, I'll ask the questions."

"Well ask, then," Nolan snapped, leaning against the wall, still a good fifteen feet away from them. Voices echoed in here. "I don't like standing here dripping wet."

"Yeah," Dinneck grinned. "You might catch your death."

Tulip said, "Might catch his death," and laughed to himself for a moment.

"Why don't you just walk over here, Mr. Webb . . . slowly . . . and stand next to Tulip and me."

Nolan shrugged and joined them, picked up his towel and began to dry off.

"Now, Mr. Webb, would you call it common for a journalist from Philadelphia to travel in the company of a thirty-eight caliber revolver?"

"You missed one, Dinneck. I carry two."

"You also carry ammunition, don't you? Does a reporter commonly hide a box of ammunition in the false bottom of his shaving kit?"

"You're a sharp kid, Dinneck. Why does a sharp kid like you dress in the dark?"

Tulip said, "I think he's a smart-ass."

Dinneck nodded. "I think you're right." Dinneck back-handed Nolan and Nolan instinctively leveled Dinneck with a right cross to the mouth.

Dinneck pushed himself up off the slippery tile floor and touched his bloodied lips. His face turned a glowing red. He motioned to Tulip, who drew the .45.

Nolan said, "That's a noisy gun, friend."

Dinneck said, "What the hell's a little noise between friends? Our car is just down the steps. We can pump a slug into you and be gone so fast your body'll still be warm by the time we're snug in bed."

Nolan's mouth formed his tight smile. "Together?"

Tulip slapped the .45 against the side of Nolan's head. Nolan moved fast enough to lessen the blow, but fell back against the wall just the same, his head spinning. He wiped blood from his ear and thought bad thoughts.

Dinneck said, "We heard you were a newspaper reporter, Mr. Webb, is that right?"

"It's a magazine, and go fuck yourself."

Tulip started back toward Nolan with the .45 in hand and Nolan sent a fist flying into Tulip's gentle mouth. Tulip yiped and clubbed Nolan with the .45 again and kicked him in the back as he went down. From the floor Nolan could see Tulip spitting out a tooth. Just then Dinneck kicked Nolan in the kidney and pain won him.

He opened his eyes a few seconds later and saw Dinneck standing above him, contemplating kicking him again. Nolan grabbed Dinneck by the right heel and heaved him, hard enough, he hoped, to land Dinneck on his tail bone, snap it and kill him. But Tulip was there to brace Dinneck's fall, and train the .45 on Nolan's head.

Nolan reached for his towel and, sitting in a puddle of pool water and his own blood, cleaned off his face while Dinneck spat questions.

"What were you nosing around the Big Seven for? What did Hal Davis tell you?"

Nolan said, "Ask Davis."

Dinneck said, "He cut out. Last he was seen was talking to you. We checked his apartment and all his things were gone. His car, too. Didn't even leave a forwarding address at the *Globe*. Why did you visit George Franco?"

"You want the truth?"

"Yeah, try the truth for a change."

"I'm doing a story on the Chelsey hippie scene. For my magazine. I heard rumors that Franco was a racket boss peddling LSD to the college crowd."

Dinneck and Tulip glanced at each other as if they almost believed Nolan's story.

Dinneck said, "I can just about buy you as a reporter, Webb . . . just about, but not quite. I picture you more as a man running. That's the way you travel, anyway. Or hunting, maybe. Which are you, Webb? Hunter or hunted?"

"Maybe I'm neither," Nolan said. Or maybe both.

"Two .38's. Half a dozen boxes of cartridges. Unmarked clothing, not a laundry mark or a label or anything. Rented car. No address beyond Earl Webb, Philadelphia, on the motel register. Not any one thing to identify you as a living human being."

"So what?"

"So . . . so I begin to think you're a dangerous man, Mr. Webb. And I don't think your presence in Chelsey benefits my employers."

Nolan said, "What do I get? Sunrise to get out of town?"

"You're a man with a sense of humor, Mr. Webb. Maybe you'll like this, just for laughs . . ."

Nolan rose up, his muscles tensed, his back arched like a cat's.

"Tulip, toss me the .45 and we'll give Mr. Webb here a swimming lesson."

As the ox was handing the gun to Dinneck, Nolan snapped his towel in Dinneck's face like a whip. It made a loud crack as it bit flesh. Dinneck clutched his face and screamed, "My eyes! My God, my eyes!"

The .45 skittered across the tile floor. Nolan leaped for it, grabbed it. He whirled and saw Tulip coming like a truck. He waited till the ox was a foot away, then smacked the barrel of the .45 across Tulip's left temple. Tulip cried out softly and pitched backward, stumbling into the pool; he hit the water hard but got lucky and didn't crack his head on the cement. Water geysered upon the big man's impact. He wound up in the shallow section, the top half of him hanging over the side of the pool, semi-conscious, his petal-like mouth sucking for air.

Dinneck was on the floor, screaming, fingers clawing his face.

Nolan slapped him. "Shut the fuck up, before the whole motel's in here."

Dinneck quieted, still a blind man, his eyes squeezed together and his face slick with tears.

"Who sent you, Dinneck?"

"I'll . . . I'll never tell you . . . you lousy cocksucker!"

Nolan seized Dinneck by the scruff of the neck and dragged him over to the pool. Nolan knelt him down and said, "Now I'm going to ask you some questions."

Dinneck kept swearing at Nolan and Nolan pushed Dinneck's head under water for sixty seconds. Dinneck came up gasping for air.

"Who sent you, Dinneck? George?"

"You son-of-a-bitch, Webb, goddamn you . . ."

Nolan put him back under for another minute. When he brought Dinneck back up he had quit talking, but his breath was heavy and his unconsciousness only a ruse.

"Did George Franco send you?"

Dinneck kept his eyes closed, tried to act unconscious.

"The next time I put you under," Nolan said, "you won't be coming back up."

No response.

Nolan shrugged and pushed Dinneck toward the water. Dinneck screamed, "No!" and Nolan hesitated before dunking him again, holding him an inch above the water.

"Who, Dinneck?"

"Not George, he doesn't know anything about this . . . George claims he never saw you!"

"You still haven't said who, Dinneck."

"Elliot, his name is Elliot! He's the one in charge . . . George doesn't have any power."

Nolan released Dinneck and the man fell in a heap at the pool's edge.

Nolan grabbed up his towel, slung it around his shoulders and headed for the door. His cigarettes were in a small puddle in the corner so he let them lay.

"You . . . you gonna leave us? Just like that?"

Nolan turned toward the voice. Tulip, coming out of his stupor, was standing in the pool, looking puzzled and wet.

"I'm not going to kiss you good night."

Tulip, dripping wet, looking ridiculous, pouted.

"And get out of those clothes, Tulip. You'll catch your death."

Tulip crawled out of the pool. He was hefting his friend Dinneck over his shoulder as Nolan left.

Back in the room, door locked, Nolan laid a loaded .38 on the nightstand by his bed, then washed up and treated his head wounds. Next time he wanted to relax, he thought bitterly, he'd take a hot shower. Hell with swimming.

He was asleep when his head hit the pillow.

4

She wore a black beret, had dark blonde hair and was smoking a cigar. She was looking into the sun, squinting, so it was hard to tell if her features were hard or soft. Her body was bony, though she had breasts, and she was leaning against a '30's vintage Ford, holding a revolver on her hip. The woman was staring at Nolan from a grainy, black-and-white poster that was a yard high and two feet wide.

The poster was tacked onto a crumbling plaster wall in a room in what had once been a fraternity house. No one Nolan spoke with in the house seemed to know what fraternity it had been—just that about four years before the frat had been thrown off campus for holding one wild party too many—and since had been claimed by assorted Chelsey U males on the hippie kick. The fraternity symbols over the door were Greek to Nolan.

The room in which Nolan stood staring back at the stern female face was inhabited by a Jesus Christ in sunglasses and blue jeans. Underneath a beard that looked like a Fuller Brush gotten out of hand, the thin young man sported love beads and no shirt. Outside of the beard and shoulder-length locks his body was hairless as a grape.

"Doesn't she just blow your mind?"

Nolan said, "Not really."

"Bonnie Parker," the young man said with awe. He wiped

his nose with his forearm. "Now there was a real before-her-time freak."

"Freak?"

"Right, man. Before her time. She and that Clyde really blew out their minds, didn't they?"

"They blew minds out, all right."

"Don't believe what the press says about them, man! They were alienated from the Establishment, persecuted by society, victims of police brutality."

"Oh." Nolan glanced at the poster next to Bonnie Parker's which was a psychedelic rendering in blue and green; as nearly as he could make out, it said, "Love and Peace Are All."

"Some of the other freaks got pictures of the movie Bonnie up on the walls. Not me. I insist on the genuine article."

"Swell," Nolan said. He lit a cigarette and said, "Got a name?"

"Me?"

"You."

Jesus thought for a moment, scratched his beard. "I'm called Zig-Zag."

"Good," Nolan said. "You're the one I was looking for."

Nolan strolled around the room, glanced at other posters hanging on the deteriorating green plaster walls. Dr. Timothy Leary. Fu Manchu For Mayor. The Mothers of Invention. Kill a Commie For Christ.

There were some paperback books in one corner, several ashtrays scattered around, a few blankets by the window. Alongside one wall a radiator spat underneath Dr. Leary's picture. The air was singed with insense.

"Irene Tisor," Nolan said. He looked out the window and watched the Chelsey River reflect the sun.

"What?"

"Irene Tisor. Did you know her?"

The mass of hair nodded yes.

"What happened to her?"

"Bad trip."

"Bad trip?"

"A down trip, straight down."

"Fell?"

"I wasn't there, man. Nobody was there but her . . . and she must've not been all there herself."

"What's the word?"

"Huh?"

"What do people say about it?"

"Nothin' . . . just that Irene thought she could fly. Guess she couldn't. Bummer."

"Was she a friend of yours?"

"So-so."

"How'd you know her?"

"She hung around the Third Eye. We talked."

The Third Eye was a nightclub frequented by Chelsey's would-be hippie element. The local underground newspaper was also called the Third Eye and the club was its editorial headquarters. Zig-Zag was the sixth person Nolan had spoken to that morning, and all had mentioned Irene as a regular at the Third Eye.

"What'd she like to talk about?"

"Life."

"Life."

"That's right, man. Philosophy one-oh-one."

"What's she think of it?"

"Of what?"

"Life. What'd she think of it?"

Zig-Zag flashed a yellow grin. "Groovy."

Right.

"Was Irene Tisor one of you?"

Zig-Zag flashed the grin again. "I give, man. What am I?"

"Whatever the hell you call it. Hippie."

"I'm not a hippie, that's a label hung on my generation by a biased press!"

"Flower child, love generation, freak, whatever. Was she one of you?"

"Well, in spirit, man . . . but in spirit only. There's a lot of us, we live kind of foot to mouth, know what I mean? We don't want for much, but hell, we don't want much."

"Irene lived pretty good?"

"Better than that. She had an apartment, I hear, with that straight Trask chick."

"But she was thick with your crowd?"

"She sympathized. She heard the music, all right, she just couldn't take her clothes off and dance."

"She heard enough to dance off a building." Nolan walked over to Dr. Leary's picture. Down the hall somebody was playing a Joan Baez record, and though Nolan didn't recognize the voice and was no judge of music, he knew what he didn't like. Nolan ground out his cigarette in Leary's bleary left eye.

"Hey, man, what the fuck you doin', there!" Zig-Zag got up and started toward Nolan, flexing what muscle there was on his skeletal frame.

Nolan's mouth became a humorless line. "You're the love generation, remember?"

Zig-Zag brushed the ashes off Leary's face and said, "What is it buggin' you, man? You come in here all straight and polite, then you get nasty. What's *buggin'* you?"

"Irene Tisor is dead. I want to know why."

Zig-Zag shrugged. "Anybody can pull a bad trip, man."

"Wasn't she a 'straight,' like me?"

"She wasn't all *that* straight, man. But I admit I never heard of her taking a trip before this. She got a little high once in a while, blew some pot, all right, but that's all I ever saw her take on, besides a guy or two."

"Did she take you on, Zig-Zag?"

"Naw, we just shot the shit. But there's a guy in the band at the Third Eye she saw pretty regular."

"What's his name?"

"Broome. Talks with an English accent, but it's phony."

"Broome. Thanks."

Nolan turned to leave, then stopped and said, "Pot cost much around here? LSD and the rest, it sock you much?"

"Cost of living's high, man. Somebody's making the bread in this town."

"How about you, Zig-Zag? Your old man, what kind of business is he in?"

"My old man? He's a banker."

"I see. Where?"

"Little town north of Chicago."

"You get this month's check okay?"

"Huh? Oh. All right, so he sends me a little bread to help out. Big deal."

Nolan nodded to Bonnie Parker's picture. "You're lucky Bonnie and Clyde *were* before their time, Zig-Zag."

"Huh?"

"They were in the banking business, too." Nolan turned and left the room, went down the stairs and out the ex-frat.

5

It was almost noon now and Nolan, sitting behind the wheel of the Lincoln, looked back on a morning of interviews in Chelsey's quote hippie colony unquote. It had gotten him nothing more than a few scraps of information and a bad taste in his mouth.

He glanced over Sid Tisor's notebook of information on daughter Irene. He had gone through the six male names in the notes—Zig-Zag and five others like him, and now all that remained were the two female names, Lyn Parks and Vicki Trask. There were probably dozens of Irene's friends her father hadn't known about—all Tisor had was a handful of names culled from Irene's occasional letters.

Lyn Parks lived at the Chelsey Arms Hotel. Nolan parked a block away and walked toward it, passing several clusters of long haired men and women wearing the latest thing in wilted flowers, plastic love beads and Goodwill Store fashions. The block was run-down but distinctly not tenement—second-hand stores, burger joints, head shops—though in Chelsey, Nolan had a hunch this would be as close to a slum as he would get.

The Chelsey Arms Hotel had seen a better day. Its theater-style marquee bore faded red lettering that didn't spell anything, and there was a worn carpet leading to double doors which said CAH proudly but faintly. Once in the lobby Nolan saw that the Arms was somewhat ramshackle but hardly in danger of being condemned; he'd stayed in worse. A desk clerk, in a rumpled gray suit, seemed to be trying to decide whether Nolan was a cop, or a salesman looking for female companionship.

There were Chelsey-style flower children all over the lobby, and Nolan sat in a chair across from two of them who were curled as one on a couch. Then he noticed the man standing by the cigar counter, pretending to look over the paperback rack.

Tulip.

Nolan got up and strolled to one of the pay phones to make his first contact with Vicki Trask. He would have to lose Tulip before he met with the girl, Irene's roommate, the most important name on Tisor's list. Nolan didn't imagine it would make too great a first impression to have Tulip barge in and turn his visit into a brawl.

He looked her number up in the book, dropped a dime in the slot and dialed.

A soft but somehow icy voice answered. "This is Vicki."

"Miss Trask, my name is Earl Webb. I'm a friend of Sid Tisor, Irene's father."

"Yes, of course. How is Mr. Tisor?"

"He's upset about his daughter."

"Well, I can understand . . . please send him my deepest sympathy."

"I'm afraid I'm asking for more than sympathy, Miss Trask."

"Oh?"

"I'm an investigator and I'm looking into Irene's death. As a favor to Sid."

"I see . . . that's generous of you, mister, uh . . . what was it?"

"Webb."

"Well, Mr. Webb, are you trying to say you'd like to see me and talk about Irene?"

"Yes."

"Right now I'm on my lunch break and I'll be going back to work in a few minutes, so . . ."

"Where do you work?"

"I'm a clerk at the bank."

"Would dinner be possible?"

"Mr. Webb, I don't even know you . . ."

"I'm ugly as sin. How about dinner?"

The voice till now cold turned warm in a gentle rush of laughter. "I must admit your voice is very intriguing . . ."

"What do you say?"

" . . . all right."

"Good."

"Might I suggest the Third Eye? The food isn't bad, the drinks are suitably damp. And you could do a little investigating on the side. That's where Irene spent much of her spare time, you know."

"That'd be fine. Stop by at seven?"

"Okay. See you at seven. Dress casual."

She hung up.

Nolan nearly smiled. A touch of promise in that voice? He glanced over at Tulip, who stood at the cigar stand engrossed in "Modern Man."

Nolan stepped in an elevator, said, "Fourth floor," to the elderly attendant. He wondered what Lyn Parks would look like. He wasn't worried about Tulip. If Tulip cared to join him, that would be Tulip's problem.

He knocked on door 419 and immediately heard movement inside. A voice cried out, "Come on in, it's open." A feminine voice.

Nolan opened the door.

The walls, pink crumbling plaster, were covered with posters and flower power graffiti. Doc Leary put in another appearance, Bonnie and Clyde Barrow (Warren Beatty/Faye Dunaway version this time) again rode the plaster. Also W. C. Fields, Mae West, a Fillmore Ballroom poster in purple announcing Moby Grape and the Grateful Dead, and several home-made efforts, including "Legalize Pot" and "If It Feels Good, Do It." There were two bubbling "lava" lamps—one red, one blue.

Nolan sat on the bed, a bare mattress with a single crumpled blanket on it. He smoked a cigarette. The girl was in the john, making john noises. He sat and smoked and waited for her. For two minutes he stared at a chest of drawers that had been stripped of varnish and assaulted with red, green and blue spray paint.

The girl came in and was naked.

She held two small jars of body make-up in one hand, one yellow, one green, and was dabbing a tiny paint brush in the jar of yellow. There was a towel over her shoulder and her body dripped beads of water.

She said, "Oh, hi."

Nolan said, "Hello."

She appeared to be painting a yellow daisy around her navel. When he noticed this Nolan also noticed a few other things about her. Her stomach was attractively plump and her legs were long and well-fleshed. Her breasts were firm and large, with copper-colored nipples. Her face was scrubbed and pretty, surrounded by white-blonde hair cut in lengths and hanging down to partially conceal her full breasts. Her pubic triangle was dark brown.

"Have we met?" She asked, frowning in thought but not displeasure.

"No."

"Did you lock the door?"

"No."

"Lock it."

"I'm here to talk, Miss Parks."

"We'll see. Lock the door."

Nolan got up and night-latched the door. He returned to the bed and sat back down. The girl sat beside him and crossed her legs and worked on the daisy that was now half-way encircling her navel. He offered her a cigarette and she bounced up after an ash tray and came back and accepted it. He watched her alternately puff on the cigarette and stroke her stomach with the tiny brush. Her skin was pearled with moisture from the shower, her flesh looked soft, pink . . .

"I don't pay," Nolan said.

"I don't charge."

Nolan drew on the cigarette and collected his thoughts. Lyn Parks stunned him a bit. He'd never met a girl who paraded around naked painting flowers on her stomach. He glanced at her again and saw the sun spilling in the window on her white-blonde hair. She smiled like a madonna.

"Lyn . . . okay I call you Lyn?"

"Call me anything you like."

But shy.

"Lyn, did you know Irene Tisor?"

"Yes. You have nice grey eyes, do you know that?"

"Were you a friend of hers?"

"I knew her, that's all. Your shoulders sure are broad."

"Did you hear anything strange about her death?"

"She took a bad trip. Have you ever been eaten alive?" She licked a pink tongue over her lips.

"Ever see her at the Third Eye?"

"All the time. Do you believe in free love?"

"Who's Broome?"

"Lead singer with the Gurus."

"The Gurus?"

"The band at the Eye. Don't you like girls, mister?"

"Did Broome and Irene Tisor see a lot of each other?"

"Broome sees a lot of a lot of girls. You seeing enough?"

"Enough. Was Irene a regular tripper? What'd she take, LSD or STP or speed, or what?"

"I don't know, none of it regular, I guess. Aren't you interested in me at all?"

"I'm busy right now. Irene Tisor is dead and I want the details."

She stroked the back of Nolan's neck. "Why?"

"I'm writing a story on her."

"Why not write a story on me?"

"We'll see."

"How do you like my daisy?" She had completed the flower and had added a green stem extending from her navel to the edge of the thatch of triangular brown.

Nolan got up, dropped his cigarette to the floor and ground it out with his toe. "Thanks for your trouble."

"No trouble. You're not going, are you?" She followed him to the door.

"That's right."

"So you're a writer, huh?"

"Yes."

"What's your name?"

"Webb."

"I guess you must not find me attractive, Mr. Webb."

"You're attractive."

"Well then, Mr. Webb, come on, what's to be afraid. It's free."

Nolan undid the night latch. "What if I were a killer?"

She stayed surface-cool but her eyes reflected a touch of

fear. But just a touch. "What if you were?"

He couldn't figure her. Well, if she didn't scare easy, maybe she could be offended. "Ever hear the term clap? And I don't mean applause."

But that didn't phase her, either. She just stretched her arms above her head and gave him another look at her lush breasts. She said, "It's your loss."

Nolan said, "Maybe."

"You'll be back."

He said, "Maybe" again and went out.

He stood staring at the closed door. Was she for real? Did she really have the guts to let a stranger in her room and stroll around naked for him, offering him a piece of tail like it was a piece of candy?

Nolan shook his head. She couldn't be on the level, she couldn't have that kind of nerve.

But he'd remember her room number. She was right that, one way or another, he probably would be back.

6

Dinneck, who was in the john hiding in the shower, heard the door close behind the man he knew as Webb. Lyn Parks, still naked, came in and said, "Okay, lover boy, you can come out now."

Dinneck stepped out of the stall, pleased to be freed from the damp, claustrophobic cell. He shook some of the moisture from his wrinkled, uncomfortable gold sportcoat and leaned his pork-pie hat back and scratched his head. As he slipped his .45 back into its shoulder holster, he glanced at Lyn Parks as she stooped nakedly to pick up her underwear. "That's a sweet ass you got there, honey."

She sneered at Dinneck as she wiggled into her panties. "It's sweet all right, but you'll never taste it."

Dinneck laughed harshly and spat in the can. "So . . . your love child trip ends when that creep Webb cuts out."

"Don't try to talk like a hippie, Dinneck," she said, pulling on ski pants that left her bare to the waist. "The only thing remotely hippie about you is your fat ass."

A low blow, but just the same Dinneck flashed her what he considered to be his most charming smile. "Look, honey, you just made an easy fifty bucks, didn't you? I mean, you didn't even have to come across for Webb, just flirted a little and painted your cute tummy a flower. Now, wouldn't you like to make an extra twenty-five for something *really* worth your while?"

She snapped her bra across Dinneck's face and one of the metal snaps bit his cheek. "You were sent here to protect me, you little bastard, not to make passes. Now get the fuck out of here."

"What's eating you!"

"Not you, dork." She whirled out of the john, hastily fastening the hooks on the bra.

Conceited little bitch, Dinneck thought, rubbing his cheek. He followed her out into the shabby mass of posters and pop art that was her apartment. He strolled over to the window and saw Webb leaving the Arms and heading down the street toward the dark blue Lincoln. In ten seconds he saw Tulip pick up Webb's tail.

Dinneck looked back at Lyn Parks who was lying on the bed in ski pants and bra, sticking her shapely ass out at him in defiance, or so it seemed to Dinneck. She was staring at the door in a wistful sort of way, apparently wishing the man called Webb—whom she'd been paid to seduce and pump for information when he came calling on her—had taken her up on her offer.

Bitch, Dinneck thought. What the hell was it to her? She could obviously use the extra twenty-five he'd offered her. What was the difference if she gave Dinneck a quick roll in the hay?

"I suppose," Dinneck said bitterly, gnawing on a toothpick, "it's something else again when Broome tells you to diddle than when you diddle on your own."

"Oh," she said, not bothering to look back at him, "are you still here?"

Dinneck wanted her and he wanted her bad and he wanted her bad right now. "All right, baby, fifty bucks, that's tops, fifty bucks!"

"Take your fifty bucks and stick it."

"You bitch, you little bitch, if Broome okays Webb, why the hell not me?"

"What gives you the idea Broome okayed it?"

"You're Broome's woman, aren't you?"

"Part-time. I'm my own woman full-time."

"Well, if Broome didn't ask you to give Webb the treatment, who the hell *did?*"

"The same guy that sent you, dummy."

"You mean Elliot?"

"That's right. God, you're brilliant."

Elliot had sent Dinneck to the girl that morning, to watch over her in case Webb got rough when he came calling. Late the night before, after washing their wounds from the pool battle with Webb, Dinneck and Tulip had reported their findings from the ransacking of Webb's motel room to Elliot. In a notebook in Webb's suitcase had been a list of names, one of which had been Lyn Parks. Since Lyn Parks supposedly belonged to Broome, one of Elliot's hippie-town peddlers, Dinneck had assumed Elliot had gotten Broome's permission before unleashing the Parks girl on Webb. Of course, Broome was a pretty weird character and probably wouldn't give a damn who did what to his woman.

Dinneck chewed on his toothpick, thought for a while longer, then said, "How do you happen to do direct business with Mr. Elliot?"

"We're acquainted."

"You sell your goodies to him, too, do you?"

"I don't *sell* myself, scumbag. I might rent out now and then, but as far as you're concerned there's no vacancy."

"Your business connection with Elliot wouldn't have anything to do with a certain 'One-Thumb' Gordon, now, would it?"

"How did you know that, you little bastard?" The girl was

surprised to hear the name, as she should be, because it was the name of her father, who was an associate of the Boys. It was a well-kept secret that she was the uncontrollable offspring of Victor "One-Thumb" Gordon. She had threatened to expose her daddy's Family ties unless he left her alone but well provided for.

"How the hell did you know about that?" She asked again.

Dinneck said, "Shut up, shut your damn mouth," and wiped his sweaty forehead.

What a goddamn fool mistake *that* was, he told himself, letting information slip like that! He had gotten mad at the bitch and let his temper flare up and expose a piece of his cover. He had to remember to play smalltimer, and he hadn't had any trouble in playing it till now. But if any of them—especially Elliot or anyone close to Elliot—saw through him, then he was washed up. If Elliot didn't get him, Dinneck had no doubt his other employers would.

And that Webb, that son of a bitch, had he seen through the hick routine? He remembered the swimming pool and how Webb had held him under water till his lungs had nearly burst. Where had he seen that face before? As soon as he took care of his job in Chelsey, Dinneck promised himself he would take care of that bastard Webb. Whoever he really was.

Dinneck walked over to the bed and looked at the girl and thought to himself that if it wasn't for the lousy clothes and the stooge role he'd had to assume, he might have gotten into that sweet bitch. As it was, the beautiful piece was sitting on the bed wishing she had made it with Webb.

"When you turned me down, sugar," Dinneck said easily, "you missed something real fine."

She kept her eyes fixed on the door. "I heard about you, needle dick. Remember a certain blonde waitress at the Eye?

She says you don't fuck for shit, and I believe her."

Dinneck snarled and swung at her. She ducked and shot a small, sharp fist into his adam's apple. While he stood choking with his hands wrapped around his throat, he saw her go to the dresser, pull open a drawer and withdraw a mostly empty vodka bottle. She broke it over the edge of the dresser and turned it into a formidable weapon. She held it up in a very unladylike manner, the slivers of glass catching bits of light and reflecting it around the room.

She said, "You're going to leave now, and you're going to leave lucky that I don't call Elliot and tell him about the crap you've been giving me. The next time you come inside kicking range of me, you'll leave wearing your balls for earrings."

Dinneck choked some more and shuffled out.

She was a bitch, all right, he thought, but she was a tough bitch.

Dinneck, in the lobby, tossed away the toothpick and fought the sour taste in his mouth with a cigarette. He rubbed his throat gently, thought about how much fun he would have within the next day or two, when he'd be free to hit Webb and leave Miss Parks begging for more. But first he had to take care of the job he'd been hired to do in Chelsey.

He stepped up to the phone, dropped in a dime and dialed Elliot's number.

Elliot was in his den reading *Fortune* when the phone rang.

It was Dinneck.

"Mr. Elliot, Webb wouldn't go for Broome's woman."

Elliot said, "He wouldn't dip into the delectable Miss Parks? Strange . . . did he give any reason for his celibacy?"

"Just smartass shit—'ever hear the word clap and I don't mean applause.' And so on."

"A man of genuine wit, apparently. Did she get *any* information?"

"No, Mr. Elliot. He still says he's a writer, with a magazine. His cover is consistent, anyway. And he keeps asking questions about that Tisor twat that did that two-and-a-half gainer off the Twill building a few weeks back. The Parks girl dodged his questions and tried to get friendly, but no go. She started in pumping for a little information, then out the door he went."

"Is Tulip still following him?"

"Yes, sir."

"Fine, Dinneck. Call back in three hours for further instructions."

Elliot hung up and rose from the desk. He stared blankly at one of the mahogany-paneled walls for a moment, then went to the doorway and called for his servant Edward, a black gentleman of around fifty.

"Yes, Mr. Elliot?"

"Ginger ale, please, Edward. With ice."

He went back to the desk and waited for the ginger ale. He drummed his fingers and glanced continually over his fireplace where, instead of a landscape, his license for real-estate brokerage hung. Behind the over-sized framed document was a wall-safe, where rested all the cash benefits netted by Elliot in the course of the Chelsey operation. Included was the last six weeks' haul, as yet uncollected by the Boys' periodic visitor.

Edward came in with the ginger ale; Elliot thanked him and spent a quarter hour sipping it. Then he rose, stripped off his herringbone suit and his pale blue shirt and his blue striped tie, and began to exercise. He exercised for twenty minutes, push-ups, sit-ups, leg lifts, jumping jacks, touching toes, knee bends, a few isometrics.

Then, exhausted, his bony frame slick with perspiration, he lay down on the black leather couch and tried to nap. And couldn't. His heart was beating quickly from the exercise and he took deep breaths to slow it but his nerves kept it going fast and hard.

He walked to his desk, opened the drawer and removed a glossy photo.

Elliot looked at the photo, at the hard, lined face and the cold eyes and the emotionless mouth.

The man in the photo was named Nolan.

And Elliot, in a cold, shaky sweat, darted his eyes from the wall-safe to the phone, wondering if he dare call Charlie Franco and tell him about the man who called himself Webb.

THREE

1

At two till seven Nolan reached the address of Vicki Trask's apartment and found himself facing a door sandwiched between the chrome-trimmed showroom windows of Chelsey Ford Sales. Just down the street was Berry Drug, the upper story of which was occupied by George Franco. As Nolan glanced in one of the windows at a red Mustang he caught the reflection of a dark green Impala creeping along the street behind him, a familiar neanderthal figure at its wheel. Nolan lifted his hand easily toward the .38 tucked beneath the left armpit of his sportscoat and looked in the reflecting glass to see what Tulip was going to do.

Tulip drove on.

Nolan straightened the collar of his pale yellow shirt, wondered absently if he should have worn a tie. He pressed the bell and placed his hand over the knob, waiting for the lock to let go. A buzz signaled its release and he pushed the door open.

She stood a full steep flight of stairs above him, displaying long, sleek legs below a blue mini skirt and she called out, "Come on up, Mr. Webb, come on up."

Nolan nodded and climbed the stairs. At the top he took the hand she held out to him and stepped into the loft apartment.

"Hello, Mr. Webb," she said warmly, "come in, please."

Her face was lovely, framed by long to-the-shoulder brown hair. She smiled invitingly and motioned him to a seat.

"Thanks," he said, refusing her gesture to take his sportscoat; she wouldn't be prepared to meet his .38.

"Drink?" she asked.

"Thanks no."

"Abstainer?"

"Just early."

"How about a beer?"

He nodded and she swept toward the bar, which was part of the kitchenette at the rear of the room. Nolan was sitting in an uncomfortable-looking comfortable modular chair; he glanced around the apartment. It was a single room, very spacious, the walls sporting impressionistic paintings, possibly originals. Overlooking the large room was a balcony divided in half between bedroom and artist's studio.

"How do you like it?"

"It's fine. You paint?"

"How'd you ever guess?" she laughed. "Yes, that's my work defiling the walls."

"Looks okay to me."

She came back with two chilled cans of malt liquor and stood in front of him, openly watching him. He took advantage of her sizing him up and did the same to her. She was a beautiful girl, the shoulder-length brown hair complemented by large, child-like brown eyes. Her body, well displayed in the blue mini and a short-sleeved clinging white knit sweater, was lean but shapely, with high, ample breasts that didn't quite go with her otherwise Twiggy-slender body. Her features were of an artistic, sensitive cast with a delicate, finely shaped nose and a soft-red blossom of a mouth.

Suddenly Nolan realized she was waiting for him to say something and the moment became slightly awkward.

He cleared his throat. "This really is a nice apartment."

"Thank you," she said, seating herself. "It's rather large for one person, and kind of spooky now that Irene is gone."

"I wonder if we could talk about Irene, if it doesn't bother you."

"No, that's all right . . . directly to business, I see, Mr. Webb?" She laughed gently. "Not much for small talk, are you?"

"No. Call me Earl, will you?"

"Of course, Earl." She looked at her hands, thinking to herself for a moment, then said, "I don't suppose small talk would fit your personality, would it? I mean, since I already feel as though I know you."

"How's that?"

"Irene spoke of you often."

Nolan's hand tightened around the glass. How could Irene Tisor have known the non-existent Earl Webb? "I never met Irene."

"Of course you have." She laughed again. "I'm afraid I'm teasing, aren't I?"

"I'm not much on humor, either."

"I don't know about that . . . Mr. Nolan."

Nolan didn't answer.

He reached over and gripped her hand and looked into her eyes and locked them with his. Fear took her face.

"I . . . I suppose . . . suppose you want me to explain."

"Yes."

She tried to smile, stay friendly, but his hard icy grip and the grey stone of his eyes froze her.

Her voice timid, forced, she said, "Irene and I, you see, were . . . extremely close . . . like sisters . . ."

She stopped to see if that explained anything, but all she got from Nolan was, "So?"

"Well, Mr. Nolan, she . . . she carried your picture in her billfold, all the time."

Nolan hadn't seen Irene Tisor for years, had hardly known her even then. There was no reason for her to carry him around with her. "Keep going, Vicki."

"She idolized you, Mr. Nolan."

"It's Webb and why should she idolize me?"

"She said she knew you when she was growing up. That you were a . . . gangster . . . but that you had gotten out. By defying your bosses."

"Suppose that's true. Suppose I did know her when she was a kid. Who was Irene Tisor that a 'gangster' would know her?"

"Her father . . . her father was one himself."

Nolan released her hand. "Okay, Vicki. Let's suppose some more. Let's suppose I did know Irene Tisor when she was growing up and her father was what you say he was. But let's also suppose I hadn't seen her for years and this part about me quitting the outfit didn't happen till eight months ago."

"She knew about it because her father helped you. Her father wasn't a very brave man, she told me, but he *had* helped you. She remembered it. It made an impression."

"How did she know?"

"Her father told her."

That was like Sid. Nolan nodded and said, "All right."

"All right what?"

"All right I believe you."

There was another awkward moment, then she managed, "Well?"

"Well what?"

"What are you going to do?"

He picked up the can of malt liquor and finished it. "Decide whether or not to kill you."

She sat back and let the air out of her as if someone had struck her in the stomach. She said, "Oh," and shut up and sat, worry crawling over her face.

"Don't sweat it," Nolan said, with a faint trace of a smile. "I'm deciding against it."

She sighed. Then, reprieve in hand, she attacked. "That's very big of you, you bastard!"

Nolan grinned at her flatly. "See? I do have a sense of humor."

She shook her head, not understanding him at all. Her eyes followed him as he rose and went to the door, opening it. She got up and joined him. She looked up at him with luminous brown eyes.

"Just my natural curiosity," she said, tilting her head, "but why?"

"Why what?"

"Why in hell did you decide thumbs up for this skinny broad? I thought hard guys like you always threw the likes of me to the lions."

Nolan hung onto the flat grin and shrugged. "I need you, for one thing."

"How about another?"

"Well, you're not the 'type' of person who ought to end up a casualty in the kind of war games I play. Anyway, I hate like hell to kill women."

"That's pretty goddamn chivalrous of you." She smiled, a mild in-shock smile. "Does that mean you plan to keep me out of your life?"

"Hardly. Later on I'm going to ask you if I can move in with you for a day to two."

That stopped her for a moment, then she got out a small, "Why?"

"I need a new place. There are some people who want to kill me and the motel I'm staying at now is getting to be a local landmark."

She touched his shoulder. "You're welcome to share this mausoleum with me for a while, Mr. Nolan."

"Webb, remember?"

"All right. Earl? Earl it is. Is that all you want? A place to stay, I mean?"

"There's more. I need information on Irene, of course."

"Of course. Is that all?"

"We'll see," he said. "You need a coat?"

"Yes, just a second." She came back with a bright pink trenchcoat and he helped her into it. She plopped a Bonnie Parker beret on her head and said, "You know the way to the Third Eye?"

He gave her half a grin. "You eat a mushroom or something, don't you?"

"Maybe I should lead the way," she said.

She led.

2

The Third Eye was a red two-story brick building along the Chelsey River, surrounded by a cement parking lot and assorted packs of young people, early teens to mid-twenties, milling about in cigarette-smoke clouds.

Nolan drove around front, in search of a parking place. He took a look at the brick building and said to Vicki Trask, who sat close by, "That looks about as psychedelic as an American Legion Hall."

She nodded and said, "Or a little red school-house."

At a remote corner of the parking lot, Nolan eased the Lincoln into a place it shouldn't have fit and said, "What the hell's the occasion?"

"You mean the crowd?"

"Yeah. It always like this?" He turned off the ignition, leaned back and fired a cigarette. As an afterthought he offered one to Vicki and she took it, speaking as she lit it from the match Nolan extended to her.

"It's always crowded on nights when they have dances. The Eye runs four a week, and this is the biggest night of the four."

"Why?"

"Tonight's the night they let in the teeny-boppers. You'll see as many high school age here as you will college, and one out of four of the hard-looking little broads you spot will be junior high."

"Why're the young ones restricted to one dance a week?"

"Because they run a bar—Beer Garden, they call it—on the other three nights. Serve beer and mixed drinks. And they serve anybody with enough money to buy."

"Drinking age in Illinois is twenty-one."

"Sure, but nobody cares. However, they don't serve booze on the night they open the dance to high school and junior high age. Chelsey's city fathers, pitiful guardians of virtue though they may be, even *they* would bitch about the Eye serving booze to that crowd."

Nolan nodded and drew on the cigarette. He looked out the car window and stared blankly at the river. He watched the water reflect the street lights that ringed the entire area. The suggestion of a smile traced his lips.

"What are you thinking, Earl?"

"Nothing."

"Come on . . . don't tell me you couldn't use a friend. You're not *that* different from everybody else. Spill some emotion."

Nolan shifted his eyes from the river to the glowing tip of his cigarette. "Emotion is usually a messy thing to spill."

She edged closer, putting a warm hand against his cheek. "I'm lonely, too, Nolan."

His jaw tightened. "It's Webb."

She shook her head, turned away. "Okay, okay. Be an asshole."

He opened the car door and she slid out his side. He paused for a moment and looked out at the river again. It had reminded him of a private place of his, a cabin he maintained along a lake in Wisconsin, near a resort town. It was one of several places he kept up under the Earl Webb name, for the times between, the times of retreat from the game he played with the Boys. Even Nolan had need for moments of solitude, peace. He hadn't meant to hurt Vicki Trask, but he didn't know her well enough yet to share any secrets.

They walked along the riverfront, casually making their way toward the building a block away. They walked where the river water brushed up easily against the cement, lapping whitely at their feet. In spite of himself, Nolan found his hand squeezing hers and he smiled; she was lighting up warmly in response when Tulip stepped out from between two parked cars.

A scream caught in Vicki's throat as she watched the apeish figure rise up and raise his arm to strike Nolan with the butt of a revolver.

Nolan dropped to the cement, the gun butt swishing by, cutting the air, and shot a foot into Tulip's stomach. Tulip bounced backward and smashed against a red Chrysler, then slid to the pavement and lay still. Nolan picked the gun from Tulip's fingers and hefted it—a .38 Smith and Wesson. Tulip made a move to get up and Nolan kicked him in the head. Tulip leaned back against the Chrysler and closed his eyes.

Nolan shook his head, said, "When they're that stupid, they just don't learn," and tossed the gun out into the river.

They walked on toward the Eye, Nolan behaving as if nothing had happened. When they were half a block away from the entrance, she managed to breathlessly say, "Did . . . did you *kill* him?"

"Tulip?"

"Is that his name? Tulip?"

"Yes, that's his name, and no, I didn't kill him. I don't think."

She looked at him in fear and confusion and perhaps admiration and followed him toward the Eye.

There was a medium-sized neon sign over the door. It bore no lettering, just an abstract neon face with an extra eye in the center of its forehead. From the look of the brick, Nolan judged the building wasn't over a year old. The kids milling about the entrance were ill-kempt, long-haired and smoked with an enthusiasm that would have curdled the blood of the American Cancer Society. Nolan saw no open use of marijuana, but he couldn't rule it out—most all the kids were acting somewhat out of touch with reality.

Inside the door they pushed through a narrow hallway that was crowded with young girls, most of them thirteen-year-olds with thirty-year-old faces. One, who could have been twelve, extended her non-existent breasts to Nolan in offering, giving him a smirky pouty come-on look. Nolan gave her a gentle nudge and moved past with Vicki through the corridor.

At the end of the hall they came to a card table where a guy sat taking money. He looked like an ex-pug, was around thirty-five and had needed a shave two days before. Nolan looked at him carefully and paid the two-fifty per couple admission. Nolan smiled at the ex-pug, a phony smile Vicki hadn't seen him use before, and moved on. Nolan followed Vicki as she went by a set of closed, windowless double doors, then trailed her down a flight of steps.

"Where the doors lead?"

"To the dance floor and Beer Garden."

"Oh."

She led him through two swinging doors into a shoddy room, cluttered with a dozen wooden tables.

"This it?" Nolan asked.

"Don't let it fool you," she told him, leading him to a small table by the wall, "the food's not bad at all."

Nolan looked around. The room was poorly lit and the walls concrete, painted black. The naked black concrete was partially dressed by pop-art paintings, Warhol and Lichtenstein prints and a few framed glossies, autographed, of big-time rock groups like the Jefferson Airplane and Vanilla Fudge. The tables were plain wood, black-painted and without cloths, and each was lit with a thick white candle stuck down into a central hole. The far end of the room, the bar, was better lighted, and the doors into the kitchen on either side of it let out some light once in a while. Other than that the room was a black sea of glowing red cigarette tips.

Nolan lit a fresh cigarette for both of them and they joined the sea of floating red spots.

"You notice the guy taking money as we came in upstairs?"

She nodded. "The one who looked like a prize-fighter?"

"That's the one."

"What about him?"

"I used to know him."

"What? When did you know him?"

"A few years back. In Chicago." He looked at her meaningfully.

"You mean you knew him when you worked for . . . ah . . ."

"Yeah."

"Did he recognize you?"

"Hell no," Nolan said. "He doesn't recognize himself in a mirror. Punchy. Surprises the hell out of me he makes change."

"What's he doing here?"

Nolan stared out into the darkness and said, "You tell me."

"How?"

"Start with the man who runs this place."

"The manager, you mean?"

"Not the manager. The owner."

"As a matter of fact . . . I *have* heard the owner's name. I've heard Broome mention it. It's Francis, or something like that."

"Franco?"

"Yes, I think that's it."

Nolan withheld a smile. "Fat George."

"I believe his first name is George, at that."

A waitress came to the table, put down paper placemats and gave them water and silverware. She handed them menus and rolled back the paper on her order blank.

Vicki asked for a steak sandwich, dinner salad and coffee, and Nolan followed suit. They ordered drinks for their wait, Vicki a Tom Collins, Nolan bourbon and water.

Nolan sat, deep in thought, not noticing the silence maintained between them until the drinks arrived five minutes later.

Vicki cupped her drink, looking down into it, and said, "Do you want me to talk about Irene now?"

"That'd be fine."

"Well . . . she was wild, Earl, not real bad or anything, but a little wild . . . I guess you could blame that on her father."

"He isn't what I'd call wild."

"But . . . isn't he . . . a gangster?"

"The deadliest weapon Sid Tisor ever held was a pencil."

"Oh. Well, anyway, Irene and I used to be quite close. You have to be, to live together, share an apartment and all. Both of us were artistic, using that same balcony studio in the apartment. Some of those paintings on the apartment walls are hers. Once in a while she wouldn't show up at night, she'd sleep over with some guy or other—no special one, there were several—but that was no big deal, I'm no virgin either. It was just this year that it started getting kind of bad. Not with guys or anything. It was when she started getting in tight with some of these would-be hippies. I went along with a lot of it, because some of these people are witty and pretty articulate. Fun to be with. For example, they meet upstairs here during the day, and put articles and cartoons and stuff together and put out a weekly underground-style newspaper, called the Third Eye."

"What you're trying to say is they're not idiots."

"Right. I'm friendly with some of them. If you leaf through some back copies of the Eye you'll see some of my artwork. But not all of these Chelsey hippies are well, benign. Some of them are hangers-on, bums, drop-outs, acid-heads. Like this Broome creep who runs the band here. Irene fell in with characters like Broome this last month or so, and I saw less and less of her . . . she was experimenting that final week or so, with pills mostly. And she kept saying, threatening kind of, that she was going to try an LSD trip."

"And?"

"She did, I guess."

"You think it was suicide?"

"Her death? I think it was an accident."

"Oh."

"You sound almost disappointed, Earl."

"To tell you the truth, Vicki, I don't give a damn one way or another. I'm just doing Sid Tisor a favor."

She looked at him, shocked for a moment. "But you knew her, didn't you? Don't you care what happened to her?"

He shrugged. "She's dead. It begins and ends there. Nothing brings her back, it's all a waste of time."

She squinted at him, obviously straining to figure him out. "You came to this stinking little town to risk your life when you think it's a waste of time?"

Nolan drew on the cigarette. "You don't understand. It's a debt I'm paying. Also, there's a chance for me to make some money off the local hoods. But I'm not doing this for me, I'm doing it for Sid Tisor. *He* cares, and that's what counts."

"Because you owe him."

"Because I owe him."

Their meals were brought to them and they ate casually, speaking very little. She watched him, beginning to understand him better.

He paid the check and they went upstairs.

3

The large gymnasium-sized room was filled with cigarette smoke, unpleasant odors and grubbily-dressed kids. Nolan stood with Vicki at the entrance and looked around, over the bobbing heads.

The black concrete walls were covered with psychedelic designs, vari-colored, abstract, formless but somehow sensual, done in fluorescent paints. The lighting consisted of rows of tubular black-light hanging from the ceiling; a strobe the size of a garbage can lid was suspended from the ceiling's center, but it was turned off at the moment. At one end of the room, to the left of the double doors, was a shabby-looking bar with an over-head sign that read "Beer Garden." It was open for business but serving soft drinks only. The other end of the room was engulfed by a huge, high-ceilinged stage piled with rock group equipment.

"Let's take a look," Nolan said.

Vicki nodded agreement and pushed through the crowd with Nolan till they reached the foot of the stage.

On stage were three massive amplifiers that looked to Nolan like black refrigerators. A double set of drums was perched on a tall platform, and various guitars were lying about as if discarded. An organ, red and black with chrome legs, faced out to the audience showing its reverse color black and white keyboard. Boom stands extended microphones over the organ and drums, and upright stands held three other mikes for the guitarists and lead singer. The voice amplification was evidently hooked up to two large horns the size of those found in football stadiums.

Vicki said, "You look at that stuff as though you know something about it."

"I do," Nolan told her. "Been everything from bouncer to manager in all kinds of clubs. You get to know musicians and their equipment."

"What does that equipment tell you?"

"They have money," he said, "and they're going to be too goddamn loud."

She laughed and a voice from behind them said, "That, my friend, is a matter of opinion."

They turned and faced a six-foot figure resembling a coat-rack hung with garish clothes. The coat-rack spoke again, in a thick, unconvincing British accent. "Aren't you going to introduce me to the gent, Miss Trask?"

She began to answer, but Nolan shushed her. "I can guess," he said, looking the coat-rack up and down.

The boy was emaciated, the sunken-cheeked Rolling Stone type that shouted drug use. His hair was kinky-curly and ratted, making him look like a freaked-out Little Orphan Annie. His face was a collection of acne past and present, and the sunkenness of his cheeks was accented by a pointed nose and deep-socketed eyes that were a glazed sky-blue. He wore a grimy scarlet turtleneck with an orange fluorescent vest and a tarnished gold peace sign hung around his neck on a sweat-stained leather thong. His pants were black-and-white checked and hung loose, bell-bottomed, coming in skin-tight at the crotch.

"You're Broome."

A yellow smile flashed amiably. "Right you are, man."

"Who picks out your threads," Nolan asked, gesturing at Broome's outfit, "Stevie Wonder?"

Broome's laugh was as phony as his English accent. "You can't bum me out, dad. I groove out at everything, everybody, everywhere. Bum *me* out? No way—I'm too happy, man."

Nolan looked into Broome's filmy, dilated eyes and silently agreed. "When you play your next set?"

Broome pulled a sleeve back, searched his wrist frantically for his watch, which turned out to be vintage Mickey Mouse on a loose strap. "In five, man, in five."

Vicki pointed Nolan to the stage where the rest of Broome's band was onstage already, four boys just as freakishly attired as Broome but apparently less wigged-out—they were tuning up, generally preparing to begin their next set. Teeny-boppers crowded in around the stage, shoving to get as close to the band as possible, and consequently pushing Nolan, Vicki and Broome into a corner to the left of the stage.

Broome was small-talking with Vicki and getting a cold-shoulder in return, Nolan having turned his back on both of them to watch the band set up. From the corner of his eye Nolan saw Broome light up a joint.

Nolan said, "That one of the things that makes you so happy?"

Broome lifted his shoulders and set them back down. "It helps a little, dad, you know?"

"I know."

Broome spoke to Vicki. "I didn't catch your friend's name, love. What is it?"

"His name is Webb," she told him. "Earl Webb."

Broome looked at Nolan and something flickered behind the gone eyes. After a moment's hesitation, he said, "I hear you get around, Mr. Webb, is that right? Do you get around?"

"I get around. How about you, Broome? Ever hear of Irene Tisor?"

Broome's face tightened like a fist. "Maybe I have, Mr. Webb, maybe I have. So what?"

"What do you know about her?"

"She's dead, haven't you heard?"

"I heard." Nolan smiled, the phony smile this time. "You just smoke that stuff, or do you sell it, too?"

"Hey, dad, I'm a *musician*."

"Yeah, right. Who sold Irene Tisor that hit of acid? Whose music was she dancing to when she did her swan dive into the concrete?"

Broome dropped his joint to the floor and stomped it out, his face a scowl and in one motion thrust his middle finger in Nolan's face defiantly.

"Make love not war," Nolan reminded him.

Broome farted with his mouth and hopped up onto the stage, joining his band, keeping an aloof air when speaking to the other members, and mumbled "One, two, test" into his mike. He gave the band four beats with his booted heel and they roared into a long, loud freaky version of a rhythm and blues number called "In the Midnight Hour." The amps screamed as if in pain, emitting feedback and distortion, while Broome tried to sound black, crouching over the microphone, as if making a kind of obscene love to it. The Gurus, his four man back-up band, seemed vaguely embarrassed by him, with the exception of the bass player, a blond youngster who wore a page-boy.

Toward the middle of the first number, somebody turned on the ceiling strobe, which flickered, flashed, making everything look like an acid-head's version of a silent movie.

Nolan said, close to her ear, "I've had enough. I won't get anything out of Broome. Not in public."

Vicki followed Nolan as he burrowed through the crowd toward the doors. Above the deafening music she shouted, "Didn't you get *anything* out of this evening?"

Nolan waited till they were in the hallway with the double-doors closed behind them before he answered. "I got a few things out of it. Saw some pot being smoked, and not just Broome. Did you smell it? Bittersweet, kind of. And I'd put a thousand bucks down that Broome is an addict."

"An addict? Can you get addicted to LSD?"

"LSD, my ass. He's riding the big horse. Heroin."

"Heroin? Are you kidding?"

"I don't kid much, Vicki. He may have Mickey Mouse on his wrist, but he's got needle tracks on his arm."

They moved back through the hallway, past the ex-pug who still didn't recognize Nolan, and out into the open air. Just as they started to walk away from the Eye, Nolan spotted a familiar face—Lyn Parks, whom he'd last seen in her apartment, as she sat naked, painting a flower 'round her navel. As she went through the door she caught Nolan's eye; she said nothing but her smile said everything.

Touch of jealousy in her voice, Vicki said, "They all give you the eye don't they, teeny-boppers on up?"

"Sure," Nolan said. "Even Broome."

They walked back to the Lincoln and drove to Nolan's motel.

4

Nolan pulled the Lincoln up to the Travel Nest's office, where through the glass he could see Barnes, the manager, at the desk inside.

"I'm going to pick up some of my things," he told Vicki, "and see to it the manager keeps my room vacant and my name on the register for the next few days."

"But you'll really be staying with me?" she asked.

"Right."

She leaned forward and caught his arm as he began to get out of the car. He glanced back and she moved forward and they kissed. A brief kiss, with a touch of warmth, of promise. He squeezed her thigh and climbed out of the Lincoln.

He had barely gone through the door and into the motel office when an ashen-faced Barnes started babbling.

"I'm sorry, Mr. Webb, they made me let them in, believe me, I couldn't help it . . ."

Nolan grabbed him by the lapel. "What the hell are you talking about?"

"Those policemen . . . they made me let them in . . ."

"What policemen?"

"The officers who searched your room last night!"

Nolan said, "Plainclothes? One tall and fat, the other short and dressed for shit?"

"That's right, that's them."

Tulip and Dinneck. That was how they had gotten into his room last night, before the pool skirmish. He hadn't bothered to check with Barnes; he'd assumed Dinneck and Tulip had gotten in on their own.

"Why the hell did you let 'em in?"

"They had a search warrant . . . I . . . I couldn't refuse them."

Nolan let him go. Of course. Of course they'd have a warrant. That financial secretary of George's, that Elliot, had a cousin for a police chief. A guy named Saunders. No trouble getting Dinneck and Tulip a police cover and a search warrant.

"Okay," Nolan said. "It wasn't your fault. But you should've told me about it later."

Barnes was dripping sweat; his bald blushing head looked like a shiny, water-pearled apple. "I was afraid, Mr. Webb, I'll . . . I'll tell you the truth. They told me you were a killer, a dangerous psychopath."

Knowing that Barnes was high-strung, scared easily and would bite almost any line fed him, Nolan leaned over the desk and looked the manager in the eye.

"What I'm about to tell you is confidential, Mr. Barnes," he said. "I need your sacred oath that you won't repeat the following to anyone."

Barnes was confused, but he nodded.

Nolan continued. "I'm an FBI special agent, investigating the illegal sale of hallucinatory drugs here in Chelsey."

Nolan could see in Barnes' face that he bought it. It rang true to Barnes; there *was* a lot of funny business about drugs in Chelsey. He believed Nolan.

Just as Nolan was ready to hand more FBI bullshit to him, Barnes' eyes lit up like flares and he began to shake.

"What's wrong?"

"Have . . . have you been up to your room yet? You have, haven't you, Mr. Webb?" Barnes shook like a bridegroom at a shotgun wedding.

"No, I haven't. What the hell's wrong with you?"

"Then you better get up there quick! I told you they made me do it!"

"What are you talking about?"

"They came in again tonight, didn't you know? I thought that was why you barged in here!"

He grabbed Barnes by the lapel again. "When?"

"Ten minutes before you came in, Mr. Webb . . . I thought you knew . . ."

"Damn!"

Nolan turned and ran to the door, spoke over his shoulder to Barnes. "Keep everybody away from that room as long as you can. No cops—they're crooked!"

"Should I call your superiors . . ."

"Don't phone anybody, don't do anything. Just keep your mouth shut."

Nolan flew out of the office, sprinted to the Lincoln and pulled open the door. "I got visitors in my room, Vicki. Sit tight till I get back. Be alert and make a fast exit if things start looking grim."

He left her with her mouth open, left before she could stop him to ask questions. He ran lightly across the motel lot and stood in an empty parking space beneath the balcony of his room. He looked up. The lights were on inside, shadows moved behind the curtained windows of the French doors leading from balcony to room. Nolan put his hands in the iron grating and his grip crumbled the crisp brown remains of the vined flowers that had climbed the trellis before the air had chilled. He tested the grating and it felt firm. He inched up slowly, the metal X's cutting into his hands; only the very ends of his shoe toes would fit into the X's, and they provided unsure footing. He edged his way up the iron trellis and in a minute and a half that seemed much longer, he found himself parallel to the balcony.

Clamping one hand tightly in one of the grating openings, Nolan withdrew his .38 from the under-arm holster and slipped one leg up and over the side of the balcony. He fought for balance, shifted his weight and landed on the balcony cat-silent.

Nolan faced the four-windowed French doors and watched the shifting shadows on the curtains. He peered through the crack between the doors and saw Dinneck sitting in a chair with his back to Nolan, tossing things from a suitcase over his shoulders, angry because he wasn't finding anything. Tulip had stripped the bed and was in the process of gutting the mattress with a stiletto.

Dumb bastards, Nolan thought. The room hadn't told them anything the night before and tonight wouldn't be any different. Well, a little different maybe.

Nolan slammed his shoulder into the French doors and they snapped open. He kicked Dinneck's chair in the seat, turning it over on him. Nolan leapt on the chair, heard bones and wood crack simultaneously, and sat on it, pinning Dinneck beneath. He leveled the .38 at Tulip, who stopped frozen, knife over mattress, with the bug-eyed expression of a punk caught stealing hub-caps.

"Raise them, Tulip," Nolan ordered. "Slow and easy and no games with the knife."

If Nolan hadn't mentioned the stiletto, Tulip probably wouldn't have remembered it, but Nolan had and Tulip did. Like a reflex Tulip whipped the knife behind his ear and let it fly. Nolan ducked, losing control of the overturned chair, and hit the floor. Behind him the stiletto quivered in the wood paneling. Nolan fired the .38 at a fleeing Tulip, caught him in the arm with the shot, which spun him around and sat him down.

That put Dinneck out of Nolan's mind just long enough for the man to crawl out from under the smashed chair and step up behind Nolan.

And when Nolan remembered Dinneck, it was too late to matter. He turned and saw the toe coming at his face and when he tried to turn away it caught him in the temple and things went black.

He woke thirty-some seconds later and stared into the barrel of his .38, which was now in Dinneck's hand. Tulip was sitting a few feet away on the partially-gutted bed, whimpering, mumbling. "Need it, Dinneck, I tell ya I need it bad . . . let's just finish him and get out, huh? What d'ya say?"

Nolan looked past the gun barrel and into Dinneck's cold, uncompromising eyes.

Nolan said, "What's Tulip need, Dinneck?"

"Shut up."

Tulip was rubbing his mutilated arm. The bullet had caught him in the lower shoulder and he was stroking below the wound. The blood from his shoulder was all over his hands and partially on his tear-streaked face, where he'd tried to wipe the moisture from his eyes. He was moaning, "I need some, gotta shoot up, need it bad, real bad . . ."

"He need a fix, Dinneck?" Nolan asked.

"Shut your goddamn mouth, Webb."

"Little shot of heroin?"

"I said shut up, you son of a bitch!"

"Where's Tulip getting his heroin, Dinneck? Is it . . ."

Dinneck interrupted Nolan by slamming the barrel of the .38 into Nolan's temple again, then smashing him across the mouth with it.

Nolan's body went limp, but he wasn't out. His mouth, his lips felt like a bloody wad of pulp, but he wasn't out. His temple ached, his head pounded, but he sat back and waited to make his move. He sat back and waited and watched Dinneck's eyes.

Tulip seemed excited, the pain momentarily forgotten. "Let *me* shoot 'im, Dinneck—let ol' Tulip put him to sleep forever—"

Dinneck smiled and shook his head. "Sorry, pal. I got a special grudge against Mr. Webb here."

Tulip stood up, clutching his bloodied arm. "*You* got a grudge! Last night that bastard set me on my ass every time I turned around, he knocked out one of my teeth, and a coupla hours ago he kicked me in the fuckin' head! Now he half shoots off my fuckin' arm and *you* gotta grudge."

"Sit down," Dinneck said, "and shut up."

Tulip sat, frowning, caressing the wounded arm again, and Dinneck consoled him with, "Take it easy, man, I'll see you get your shot, don't worry, stay cool. Let me handle it."

Nolan had been looking past Dinneck's tacky clothes and into the authority of his face, the competence of his actions, the hardness of eyes that spoke professionalism. Nolan told himself he'd misjudged Dinneck, whose dress and even manner to a degree had been calculated to elicit such misjudgment. Beyond that, Nolan saw a coldness in Dinneck, and a need to inflict pain.

"I read you wrong, Dinneck," Nolan said.

Intrigued by the comment in spite of himself, Dinneck said, "What?" Then remembering his previous commands to Nolan he said, "Just keep your mouth shut while I figure what to do with you."

"Who are you, Dinneck?" Nolan asked.

"I told you to shut your mouth."

"Tulip, how long's Dinneck been working with you? He been in town very long? How long's he been with Elliot and Franco?"

"You're only making it tougher on yourself, Webb," Dinneck told him evenly.

Tulip's face showed the strain of thought, then he said, "He's only been with us about two, maybe three months. He's somebody the Boys sent in from upstate somewhere."

Nolan looked at Dinneck again. "Who are you?"

"Just keep trying my patience, Webb, keep going at it . . ."

"You some kind of Family inside man, checking up? Just who the hell are . . ."

Dinneck's face exploded into a red mask, veins standing out on his forehead like a relief map. He raised the gun up over Nolan's head and brought it down fast.

But not fast enough. Nolan sent a splintering left that caught Dinneck below the left eye and followed with a full right swing into his throat. Dinneck rolled on his back, wrapping his hands around his throat, and he tried to scream in pain but that only made it worse. Nolan tromped down on Dinneck's wrist and the man released his grip on Nolan's .38—he'd forgotten it anyway.

Nolan stood over the sprawling figure, leveling the retrieved .38 at Tulip, who had sat back down on the bed.

"You didn't have to hit him in the throat, did you?" Tulip's voice was like a child's; he wasn't holding onto his arm anymore and the blood on it was beginning to turn a dry brown. "You didn't have to hit his throat. It still hurts him from this morning when some broad hit him there. What a hell of a place to hit him. You sure are a mean son of a bitch, Webb." Tulip shook his head.

"You and Dinneck came to the wrong man for sympathy,"

Nolan told him. "He should've got his tonsils out some other day."

"What are you gonna do now?"

Nolan didn't answer Tulip. He lifted a barely conscious Dinneck by the collar and dragged him to the can, keeping one eye (and the .38) on Tulip all the while. Nolan dumped Dinneck in the tub, turned on the shower full blast, on cold, and pulled the shower curtain down over his head.

"You sure are a mean s.o.b.," Tulip repeated.

"It'll relax him," Nolan said.

Nolan left Dinneck in the tub, shower curtains around him and shower going on full, ice-cold. Dinneck was a mass of whining, hysterical pain, fighting the shower curtain and the cold with what was left of his will. Nolan shut the bathroom door.

"I bet you could use a shot, couldn't you, Tulip?"

"Mean s.o.b., sure are a mean s.o.b. . . ."

"How long you been riding that horse, Tulip?"

" . . . mean s.o.b., you sure a . . ."

Nolan gave up on getting any information out of Tulip; at the moment the big man was practically catatonic and talking to him was a waste of time. Besides, pretty soon Barnes would get worried enough to call the cops, despite Nolan's advice to the contrary, what with the gunshot and all the violent noises that had been coming from the room. He wondered if Vicki had taken off. She should have.

He collected his things, picked his suitcase up off the floor and hastily re-packed it, got his clothes-bags too. He rubbed his temple; his head was still pounding like hell, but his balance was okay. A few aspirin would help the head as long as there wasn't concussion. His mouth was bleeding and hurt like a bastard, but he ran a hand over it and didn't think he would need stitches.

Out in the hall, he could hear a muffled Tulip in there saying "Mean s.o.b." over and over. Nolan lugged his suitcase and clothes-bags thinking he could have been a lot meaner than he'd been. He wouldn't have lost much sleep over killing that pair.

The Lincoln was indeed waiting and he walked easily over to it. Vicki was at the wheel, the engine running. He got in the rider's side, tossed his things in back.

When she saw him her eyes rolled wide and she gasped. "What happened! Your face, your mouth . . ."

"Hard day at the office," he said. "Beat it the hell out of here."

5

Sometimes, when insomnia hit him and he spent half the night fighting for sleep, Phil Saunders almost wished his wife were alive.

This was a night like that. He'd gone to bed at twelve, as soon as the late night talk show had signed off. Now it was two-thirty and he was still awake.

Yes, too bad, in a way, his wife wasn't alive any more.

At least if she were there she could have bitched him to sleep.

Now there was no one. No one to talk to, have sex with, live with. A little old fashioned nagging never killed anybody. At least you weren't alone.

Not that it was bad, living alone here. He had a nice apartment, six rooms, luxury plus. And very nicely furnished, too, in a conservative sort of way. But then, Phil was a conservative sort of person, outwardly upright, honest. But on the inside? Life had grown a sour taste lately.

A year and a half ago life had been sweet. A year and a half ago when he had been Police Commissioner of Havens, New Jersey, a legit above-board job he'd worked his ass off over the years to get. A year and a half ago his wife had been a drying-up prune he put up with out of habit and for appearance sake. A year and a half ago his affair with Suzie Van Plett, that succulent soft little seventeen-year-old, had been in full bloom.

Too bad his wife had walked in on him and Suzie that time. There's nothing like the sight of a naked seventeen-year-old blonde sitting on the lap of a naked forty-nine-year-old balding police commissioner to give a really first rate instantaneous and fatal heart attack to a fully-clothed fifty-two-year-old grey-haired police commissioner's wife. Then the reporters, the disgrace, the friends deserting him, the question of statutory rape in the air and finally the humiliating midnight escape.

His name had been different then, but it died with his wife and his reputation in Havens. He turned to his cousin, a long-time con artist going by the name Irwin Elliot. Elliot had a sweet set-up going in Chelsey, Illinois, through the Chicago crime syndicate. Cousin Elliot was good at documents and he forged the defrocked Havens police commissioner a good set of references, pulled the proper strings, opened and closed the right mouths, and the newly named Phil Saunders sprang to life, full-grown at birth. He filled the puppet role of Chelsey Police Chief and watched his cousin Elliot control the town as the brains behind another puppet, that fat fool George Franco, who was a brother of some Chicago mob guy.

It was a rich life, and an easy one.

But there would no succulent seventeen-year-olds in his Chelsey life, nor would there be, on Cousin Elliot's orders.

Just a conservatively furnished six-room apartment that even his dead wife could have brightened with her presence. At least if his wife were around there would be someone *not* to listen to, *not* to talk with.

The door buzzer sounded, startling Saunders. Then, knowing who it would be, he went to the door and opened it.

He smiled and said, "Hi, buddy," and then he noticed the .38 in his visitor's hand.

The gun went to his temple, the visitor fired and Saunders joined his wife.

Lyn Parks had been with Broome long enough. He was a lousy bed partner, he smelled bad and his manners were non-existent.

They were in the backstage dressing room at the Third Eye, and it was three o'clock in the morning. Broome had been trying desperately to get her to come across since after the band's last set and his failure was getting him angry, despite the fact that he'd shot up with horse a few minutes before and should have been feeling quite good by now.

"Get your goddamn hands off me!" She shook her head in disgust with him, with herself. "You're really a sickening bastard, Broome, and it's pretty damn revolting to me to think I ever let you touch me."

"Come on, babe, you ain't no cherry . . ." He groped for her and she was sick of it. After seeing him shoot up with H—he'd never had the poor taste before to shoot up right in front of her—she was almost physically ill with the thought of her few months of close association with the man. She was ready to move on—life with Broome and these sick creeps was worse than life with her father, "One Thumb" Gordon, a gangster who pretended respectability. She hated phonies, like her father, and she hated Broome as well, for his brand of phoniness.

"You aren't anything but a pusher, Broome," she told him bitterly. "Flower power? Some of the kids in this town are on the level with their peace and love, but you . . . you're a bum, a peddler, a cheap gangster worse than my father ever was."

"Your father? Who's your father?" Broome wasn't having much luck with trying to speak, everything was coming out slurred.

It was disgusting to Lyn, this rolling around with a doped-up lowlife on a threadbare sofa in a back-stage people closet with dirty wooden floors and graffitied walls. Broome was no threat, he was already on the verge of incoherence, sliding into dreaminess. She started for the door.

Then heard the footsteps.

Somebody banged on the door.

Fear caught her by the throat and she instinctively ducked in the bathroom, where Broome had so often shot up, his works still on the sink.

She heard Broome mumble something out there, maybe a greeting. A few more words.

Then a gun-shot.

Kneeling tremblingly, she peered through the keyhole and saw a person she recognized pocket a revolver and turn and go. She waited three long minutes before opening the closet wide enough to see Broome, lying on his back like a broken doll, his freaky blond Orphan Annie curls splattered with blood and brains, skull split by a bullet.

She puked in the sink.

She wiped the tears from her eyes, found control of her retching stomach, wondered what to do . . .

Webb.

That was it, she had to find Webb.

He could do something about this.

At least he could take her away from it . . .

She ran.

George Franco was pissed, in several senses of the word.

He sat by the window and stared down the block at the extended sign of Chelsey Ford Sales, the building he'd seen Nolan enter several times during the day—the last time around midnight with a pretty girl, a girl George thought he recognized.

It was too late to be drinking, but George was. He sat in his red and white striped nightshirt like a colorful human beach ball and nursed a bottle of Haig and Haig.

That fucker Nolan. Who did he think he was, pushing George around? And why hadn't Nolan called? One whole day gone since he and Nolan had made their pact, with Nolan saying he'd check in every now and then. Well, why the hell didn't he?

George had decided he wanted a favor from Nolan—in return for keeping quiet about the thief's presence in Chelsey. It was only fair . . . and it would be a favor that Nolan would get something out of in return . . .

George swigged the Scotch, looking out at the blank street, the naked benches by the courthouse cannons. He didn't see anybody watching him; Nolan said he had three men taking turns watching George, only now George wasn't so sure. The tower clock read three-fifteen, but George wasn't tired. He was all worked up. And he was thirsty.

It had come to him tonight, how he could use Nolan to better his position. To make his brother Charlie reconsider his opinion of George; to have some responsibility again. To get rid of that smug bastard Elliot and have the last laugh . . .

If he could only remember that girl's name! That girl who'd been with Nolan, it was *her* apartment they'd gone into!

He'd met her once in the drugstore below. She was a friendly little thing, she said she'd seen him and she guessed they were neighbors and how was he? But that was a long time ago, a year or so, and he couldn't remember . . .

Vicki something.

More Scotch. It would help him remember, more Scotch . . .

Trask.

Vicki Trask.

He waddled to the phone book, a pregnant hippo in a nightshirt, and thumbed through the pages.

Sure it was late, and Nolan would be pissed, but that was just too bad. He couldn't push a Franco! Why, George could have his brother and an army down from Chicago in a few hours, with just a snap of his fingers! He could erase Nolan, have him wiped out like a chalk drawing on a blackboard! It was that easy.

He dialed. Nolan would talk to him, he knew he would.

It rang a long while and a female voice answered. He asked to speak to Mr. Webb and she said just a minute.

He waited for Nolan to come to the phone. The female voice had been pleasant. Like his whore's, Francie, only more sincere. He'd been mean to Francie today, edgy over the thing with Nolan, and she'd walked out mad. He'd called her twice and asked her to come back and let him try and make it up to her. She'd hung up both times, but he still hoped she'd show. Maybe could patch things up with dollars and Scotch.

Then Nolan was on the phone.

"Yes, I know it's late, Mr. Nolan . . . sorry, Mr. *Webb* . . . but I have to talk with you . . . I can help you take Elliot down . . ."

There was a soft rap at the door.

George said, "Just a second, Nolan, I mean *Webb* . . . the door, I think my girl friend might be back, jus' a second."

George stumbled to the door, thinking to himself about how fine it would be to see his Francie at the moment, have a nice drink with her.

He opened the door and an orange-red blossom exploded in somebody's hand and burst George's head and he went down, a sinking barge.

FOUR

1

Nolan reached out in the darkness and stroked the sleeping girl's breast. She stirred in her sleep, a smile playing on her lips. He ran his hand under the sheet and over her smooth body, over her thighs to the flat stomach, across the soft rises of breast, nipples now relaxed, the tightness of passion a memory.

Vicki Trask's eyes opened slowly; then blinking, yawning, she said, "Are you *still* awake? It must be after two in the morning—"

Nolan flipped back the sheet. He took a gentle bite out of her stomach, nuzzling her. His lower lip cradled the dip of her navel, his upper lip tickled by the tiny hairs on her flesh.

"Salty," he said.

"Hmm?"

"You taste salty."

"I ought to," she replied. "You worked me hard enough."

"It's good for you." He moved up to her breasts and nibbled. The tips, remembering, grew taut again.

"Ouch! Take it easy!" Then she laughed and looped her arm around his neck.

He looked into her little girl face and said, "You were good, Vicki."

The faint light from a street lamp poured through a circular window into the balcony and gave her skin a glow, an almost mystical look, like a textured photograph. She sat up in bed and propped her knees up and rested her chin on them, locking her hands around her legs. She stared at him, her smile slight.

"You were wonderful," she told him. "I . . . I never felt so much a woman before." She leaned over and brushed her lips across his cheek.

"You're a woman all right," he said. Not entirely true, but she had been a lot less girl than Nolan had expected.

Boredom from the so far sleepless night mixed with the infrequency of sexual activity in his life of late tempted Nolan to go another round with the girl. She'd admitted she wasn't a virgin, but she'd been close to one, and he didn't want to press her unduly.

But then her lips were on his chest and her fingers had found their way to his back, where they were digging in. She looked at him, resting her head against his chest, her expression one of sweet shame, asking him if . . . ? He reached his arms around her and covered her mouth with his.

Twenty minutes later Nolan was sitting in the dark smoking, his back against the headboard, his mind adrift. His left arm was around her shoulder, his hand cupping a breast. The other arm rested on the nightstand by the bed, where he'd laid his un-holstered .38. Vicki had floated into sleep a few minutes before, but he remained awake beside her, thinking and smoking, smoking and thinking . . .

Around three a.m. Vicki awoke suddenly and found Nolan still sitting back against the headboard with the fourth, maybe fifth cigarette tight in his lips. His grey eyes were open, two dead coals in the darkness.

"What's the matter? What is it? Why are you still up?"

He didn't look at her. "Have to be leaving soon."

"Is it getting to be dangerous for you to stay around Chelsey, or what?"

"No, that's not it . . . it's always like that for me. It's just that I got a feeling there's nothing here that needs to be found out about Irene Tisor."

Her hands played with the blanket. "When do you have to leave?"

"Soon, I said." He had to figure a way to hit the Chelsey operation first—he had to get his hands on this Elliot guy and make his hit for the cash on hand and the hell with Chelsey and Sid Tisor's dead kid.

"Will I see you again? After you leave Chelsey?"

"Sure."

"You're not telling the truth."

There was no answer to that.

She buried her head in his chest and he felt her tears on his flesh.

He smoothed her hair. It was soft and fragrant. "Don't pretend to yourself that you want me to stay."

"What do you mean?"

"I mean I'm one or two nights in your life and that's all I am. Accept me that way."

She studied him, her eyes moist. "You know something, Nolan? No, don't object to me calling you Nolan, you're not Earl Webb you're Nolan and in my bed I'll call you Nolan if I damn well please. I have you pretty well figured out. You walk around like a mobile brick wall. So cold, the ice forms on your shoulders. And you know what you are under all that ice, Nolan?"

"You tell me."

"You're all the emotions you despise to show. You're like that gun over there. You're a hunk of metal until you get in a demanding situation, then you explode. I've been with you only a few hours, but I've seen you kick a man in the head and later come out of your motel room looking like you just wrestled a grizzly and won. And I've shared my bed with you, and you were tender enough, I guess, but that damn gun of yours remained on the nightstand beside you all the while. Anybody as violent as you, and as passionate, is a fire-bomb of emotion. Now . . . what do you think about that?"

He was silent for a moment. Then said, "I think you talk too much."

She laughed her warm laugh and nodded that she guessed he was right and leaned her head against his shoulder.

"You going to stay in Chelsey, Vicki?"

"I don't know," she said. "I have . . . have a problem or two that may keep me here."

"It's your business," Nolan shrugged.

She smiled. "I guess you think I was out of line a minute ago with my dimestore psychology. Now here I am keeping secrets from you. But . . . everybody needs a *few* secrets."

"Sure."

The phone rang.

"Who the hell would call you at this hour?"

"Nobody."

"You better get it."

"Are you here, Nolan?"

"Earl Webb is."

"Okay . . ."

"Careful," he told her. "Too goddamn late for a phone call. It's going to mean something, whatever it is."

"Even a wrong number?" she laughed.

"Answer it before they give up."

She climbed out of bed and threw a filmy negligee over her creamy-white skin. She flew down the spiral staircase that connected the balcony to the living room and grabbed up the phone, which was on the bar in the kitchenette. Upstairs, Nolan leaned back and took a cigarette from the half-empty pack and popped it into his mouth.

From below, her voice came, "It's for you, Earl."

He got out of bed, slipped into his pants and shoes and went down the spiral staircase, taking his .38 with him.

"This is Webb."

"This is George, George Franco . . ."

"What do you want, George? A little late for you to be up, isn't it?"

"Yes, I know it's late, Mr. Nolan . . ."

"Webb."

"Sorry, Mr. *Webb* . . . but I have to talk to you!"

"About what?"

"I can help you take Elliot down."

There was a hesitation at Franco's end.

"What's wrong, George?"

"Just a second, Nolan, I mean *Webb,* the door, I think my girl friend might be back. Jus' a second."

There was silence and Nolan looked at Vicki and said, "Think he's been into the cooking sherry again."

She smiled in confusion and Nolan half-grinned and the receiver coughed the sound of a gun-shot.

Nolan dropped the receiver as if it were molten and ran out the door and down the steps to street level. He wasn't wearing a jacket—just a t-shirt—and the cold air hit him like a pail of water.

From the doorway above Vicki called down, "Nolan . . . what are you doing . . . ?"

"Wait here," he said. "Somebody just got shot. Stay put, don't let anybody in but me."

"But . . ."

"Shut the door and wait, Vicki," he told her, wheeling around to face the deserted courthouse square, marked only by a few scattered parked cars whose owners lived in apartments over stores. Down the street a light was on in George's penthouse above the Berry Drug.

Nolan ran to the corner, turned and slowed into the alley. He kept the .38 in front of him and made sure the alley was empty. Then he jumped up and pulled down the fire escape and climbed to where he had used his glass cutter to get in the day before. He elbowed the cardboard patch and it gave way easily. He slipped in his hand, unlocked the window and crawled into the apartment.

There was no one inside except George, and he was over by the door, dead, his head cracked like a bloody egg.

The killer had used a .45, Nolan thought, or possibly a .38 at close range. Plugged George right square in the forehead with it. Effective. Not particularly original, but effective.

The killer hadn't bothered to hang up the phone, which was making the loud noises the Bell people use to persuade you to hang the damn thing up. Nolan slipped it onto the hook and heard sounds coming from the drug store below.

He climbed back out the window and down the 'scape and dropped silently to the ground. Cautiously he made his way around to the front of the store, wondering if the killer had made his way out yet.

Then Nolan heard tires squealing away from a curb down the street from behind him.

In the alley he found a back door, still open, where the killer had hot-footed it from the drug store to a car parked along the side street. Nolan could see it in the distance, blocks down. It was a dark blue Cadillac having no trouble at all disappearing.

He stood there for a while thinking, cold as hell and just as he was wishing he'd brought his cigarettes along, a blue-and-white squad car sidled up next to him. "Chelsey Police" was written on the door in small print, as if they were ashamed of it.

A man in a nicely-pressed light brown business suit stepped out of the squad car, flanked by two uniformed officers. The plainclothes cop had a tanned, weathered face, a shrewd, tough cop's face, and that was one of the worst kinds. The cop being a plainclothes meant he was probably one of the smartest, most experienced officers of the Chelsey force. Which didn't necessarily mean much. Nolan figured being a top cop on Chelsey's force was an honor akin to being the harem's head eunuch.

The cop motioned the uniformed pair up the 'scape and into George's apartment, everyone obviously knowing just what to expect. A few minutes after they went in, one of them, a scrubbed-faced type, looked down at the cop who was standing below with Nolan and said, "Yup."

The cop smiled. "What's that you got in your hand?"

"It's a gun."

"You got that filed with the city?"

"I got," Nolan said, stuffing the .38 in his waist band, "a closed mouth till I see a lawyer."

"I'd tell you to keep your shirt on, pal, if you were wearing one." The cop's tough face broke into a wide grin. "I sure hope you haven't fired that thing lately."

Nolan didn't say anything. Why didn't the cop take the gun from him?

The cop kicked at the loose gravel in the alley, like a kid kicking pebbles into a stream. "You might be interested to know that within the past hour, hour and a half or so, the fair city of Chelsey has been seriously blemished. Blemished by three, count them, three . . . murders. Murders committed, strangely enough, with a .38."

"Who's dead?"

"So you decided to open your mouth? I don't see any lawyers around."

"Who?"

"You're a regular owl, aren't you? Okay mister, I'll tell you. The Police Chief, one Philip Saunders, found dead on the floor of his apartment, a bullet in the head. An alleged musician at the Third Eye, one Broome, no other name known, found dead on the floor of his dressing room, a bullet in the head. And I assume we have a similar problem with George Franco, up there. You might say fat George has a weight problem—a dead weight problem."

"You might say that," Nolan said, "if you were a fucking comedian."

"You're getting nasty, mister, you aren't in any position to get . . ."

"I got an alibi."

"Swell," he said.

"An on-the-level alibi. She's got a name and everything."

The cop's mouth twisted. "You really do have an alibi, don't you?"

"That's right."

He scratched his head, shrugged. "Well, then . . . you're free to go. Nice talking to you . . . mister, uh, Nolan, isn't it?"

Nolan froze.

"It's Webb," he said. "Name's Earl Webb. From Philadelphia."

"Tell me all about it."

"You going to charge me with something?"

The cop scratched his head again. He did that a lot. "I would, but I can't make up my mind between breaking-and-entering, carrying a handgun without a permit, and, well, murder. You got a three-sided coin on you?"

"Take me in or don't take me in."

"What if I said I got a deal to make with you, mister . . . ah . . . Webb. And that if you keep your side of the bargain, I'll let you walk. Without so much as a citation for loitering. Interested?"

"Maybe."

"You got somewhere private we could go?"

"Maybe."

The cop was through talking. Now he was waiting.

"Okay," Nolan said. "Let's go."

2

The cop's name was Mitchell. Nolan introduced him to the now fully awake, fully clothed Vicki Trask, who looked much fresher than four-o'clock in the morning. She was wearing a blue and red candy-striped top and a white mini skirt.

"I'm sorry to barge in on you so late, Miss Trask." Mitchell tried to look embarrassed and was fairly successful.

"That's all right, Mr. Mitchell. Would you two like anything to drink?"

"Something soft would be fine," Mitchell told her, "if it wouldn't be any trouble."

"Cokes, Vicki," Nolan said.

The girl walked to the bar and iced two glasses. Mitchell and Nolan sat, the cop wondering with his eyes if they should begin speaking and Nolan shaking his head no. When Vicki brought them the Cokes, Nolan told her quietly to wait for him in the bedroom and she followed his command, scaling the spiral staircase wordlessly and disappearing into the balcony above.

Mitchell said, "I'll put it to you straight, Nolan. You are wanted for questioning in half a dozen states . . . Illinois one of them. Matter of fact, it's kind of a coincidence, because just this afternoon I was glancing at a bulletin on you . . ."

"Can it."

"What did you say?"

"I said can it. I'm not wanted for a goddamn thing."

The cop bristled. "Who the hell do you think you . . ."

"Okay, Mitchell. You want to haul me in?"

"I . . ."

"You don't have a thing on me."

"I have half a dozen circulars . . ."

"Bullshit."

"Now wait just a damn . . ."

"Bullshit! How'd you know who I was?"

Mitchell swallowed thickly. "Anonymous tip late this afternoon. We were told you were in town. Of course we recognized the name . . ."

"Oh? What's my real name?"

"Your real name?"

"My real name. You don't know it. How about military service? Got anything on my distinguished service medal?"

"Of course I know about your medal, what do you take me for?"

"I take you for a piss-poor bluffer," Nolan said. "When I was in the service, I got a little mad and beat the hell out of a military cop. Got a bad conduct discharge. That was under my real name, which nobody I can think of knows outside of me. And even I forget it sometimes."

"You're a real smart fella, Nolan."

"You aren't. What do you want?"

Mitchell's jaw was tight, his teeth clenched. "I could run your ass out of this town so quick, your head'd spin . . ."

"Then do it."

"What?"

"Do it. Run my ass out. Make my head spin. Put any more pressure on and I'll leave on my own." Nolan leaned forward and gave the cop a flat grin. "But I don't think you want me to leave."

Mitchell's face split into a wide smile and he helped himself to one of Nolan's cigarettes in the pack lying on the table. "Okay, Nolan. I guess I'm too used to dealing with punk kids who scare easy. You see through me like a window. You're right. I don't want you to leave."

"What do you want from me, Mitchell?"

"Your help, in a way. Look, I got no bulletins on you, but I sure as hell know about you. A lot of cops across the country've heard the scuttlebutt about you and your one-man vendetta against the Chicago outfit."

"It's no vendetta."

"I heard . . ."

"You heard wrong. I steal from them. That's it. I get a kick out of upsetting their applecarts. For money. And I'm staying alive when they send people to kill me."

"You admit you've killed?"

"I'm not going to lie to you. There's no court stenographer sitting here. I've killed in self-defense and skipped hanging around for an inquest, sure. I stick in one place that long I get dead quick."

"You don't look like the type who's afraid of much of anything."

"Only idiots fear nothing. If I can fight something, then no sweat. But you can't hold ground and fight a bomb in your room. Stay in one spot long enough and they find a way to get you."

Mitchell leaned back and smoked slowly and thought.

Nolan reached for a cigarette and said, "Make your pitch, Mitchell. Let's have it."

Mitchell smiled. "You know how long I've lived in Chelsey, Nolan?"

"No, and do you think I give a damn?"

"I was born here. It was a nice little place for a long

time, friendly, homey, very Midwest, you know? Called it the intellectual corner of Illinois, too, because of the university . . ."

"Get to the point," Nolan said. "If there is one."

"All right." Mitchell's face hardened; it was deeply lined, more deeply lined than that of the average man of thirty-five or so years. "I could make things rough for you, Nolan, if I wanted to. I could hold you long enough to find out who you are, especially since you kindly informed me of your trouble during your stay in the army. The army keeps records. Fingerprints and such. A bad conduct discharge shouldn't be hard to trace."

"If I was telling the truth," Nolan shrugged.

"I don't know what you're after, Nolan, but I know enough about you to have a general idea. You came to Chelsey to hit the Family's local set-up, right?"

Nolan just looked at him.

"Now, off the record, as they say . . . what I want is the man in charge. Give him to me. Then maybe I can start cleaning this town up a little bit."

"And you'll give me a free ride home, I suppose?"

"As long as I get the goods on the head man, you'll be free to go. With anything you might relieve him of in the way of cash."

Nolan said, "You don't have any idea who your 'head man' is?"

"I've been trying to find that out for over a year, since I first started to realize just what kind of corruption was going on here. You don't mean you already *know* who he is?"

"Found out the day I got here."

"How?"

"Never mind that. You said your police chief, Saunders, was killed tonight?"

"One of three dead . . . so far."

"Well, Saunders wasn't in charge, but he was in up to his ass."

"I knew it!" Mitchell slammed fist into palm. "That son-of-a-bitch has been crippling the force since the day he took office."

"What about the next man killed?"

"Broome? We think he was involved in some kind of narcotics ring. There was heroin in his blood stream at time of death, and we found a hypo in the room and some H. Couple hits worth."

"Broome was a junkie and a pusher and a creep. But my money says he's outside help linking Chelsey to a drug supplier."

"Broome?"

"That's right. The Boys in Chicago, the mob in New York, they wouldn't send a punk like Broome in, because he was a user. But maybe he used to work for the Chicago or New York mob before he got hooked, and still had connections to a supplier."

Mitchell was confused. "This is beginning to go over my head."

Nolan didn't like explaining things, but to handle Mitchell properly, the cop had to be told what was going on. Narcotics, Nolan told Mitchell, were hard to organize; by nature they were a sprawling thing, a pusher here, a pusher there, nothing that could be controlled easily. For years the Commission hadn't bothered even trying to control it. But the last seven, eight years, Nolan explained, had changed things: the eastern families had put on a big push to organize narcotics once and for all, and with large success.

"But it's tough to hold rein on narcotics traffic," Nolan said. "The difference is that now, if you're a non-

Commission sanctioned narcotics dealer and they find you out, you get leaned on."

"Leaned on hard?"

Nolan's look was that of a father dealing with a backward child. "The Commission of Families doesn't know how to lean soft."

"So this Commission has to authorize narcotics trafficking, or it's no go. And the Chelsey operation is an extension of the Chicago Outfit, which is a Commission member. Are you suggesting the Commission doesn't know about the narcotics trade in Chelsey?"

Nolan nodded. "And the Chicago Boys don't know it, either."

"Now I *am* lost."

"That's because you don't understand what the Chelsey operation was for. George Franco, brother of one of the Boys or not, was a big nothing. The Chelsey set-up was supposed to be a minor deal, just to give worthless George something to do, make him look good, save a little face for the Francos. But this operation is obviously making money. A lot of it. Money the Commission in New York doesn't know about. Money the Boys in Chicago don't know about. And when they find out, both the Boys and the Commission are going to be pissed. But good."

"Who's behind it? Who's getting the money?"

"Not George Franco, that's for sure."

"Then who?"

"Who brought your late police chief to town?"

Mitchell thought for a moment. "That real estate big shot. Supposed to be Saunder's cousin or something. Elliot."

Nolan nodded. "Him."

"You can't mean it," Mitchell said. "Elliot's as legit as can be . . ."

"No. He's the one. Elliot. He's your boy."

Mitchell rose. "I'll be damned if I don't believe you." His face twisted with a big grin. He shrugged and said, "Well, Nolan, since you told me all this, I guess there isn't much left for you to do. I'll go out and arrest Elliot . . ."

"Go out to Elliot's place without hard proof, Mitchell, and you're fucked. Wait around while you collect evidence, and you won't see Elliot again. Except maybe in a travelogue of Brazil."

"I can't let you go out and . . ."

"You were willing to five minutes ago. How about those murders tonight? Elliot pulled 'em, you know. Any idea what those murders were for?"

Mitchell shook his head.

Nolan grinned, his first full-out grin for a long time. "He was house-cleaning," he said. "Taking care of anyone who could spill anything that could lead Boys, Commission, cops or feds to him. And five will get you five hundred he'll be out of the country by tomorrow morning."

Nolan got up and called for Vicki. He asked her to get the rest of his clothes and she did. He sat on the sofa and checked his .38, which he stuffed into the shoulder holster under his arm. Then he slipped into the blue plaid parka and walked to the door. Mitchell stood there and didn't say a word.

"Do I have to tie you up, Mitchell?"

"No."

"Stay away from Elliot tonight."

"You going to take him?"

"Yes."

"Alive?"

"I don't know."

"I'm going with you."

"Forget it."

Mitchell fought himself, finally accepted it, saying, "If it has to be that way, all right. I guess I suggested it myself, didn't I?"

"That's right. Stay here and watch Miss Trask. She's been seen with me and could be in danger. If I need you, I'll call."

Mitchell nodded reluctant agreement and Nolan said good-bye to Vicki and went out the apartment, down the steps and to street level. He walked to the Lincoln and got in.

He heard the heavy breathing in the back seat instantly and his hand was over the butt of his .38 when he heard a voice say, "Take me with you, Webb! Let's get the hell out of this hick town."

3

"What the hell do *you* want?"

Lyn Parks crawled up off the floor in back and sat on the seat. She leaned forward, shook her head of blond hair and stroked Nolan's temple. She said, "I think you know what I want, Mr. Webb, but I don't want it in Chelsey."

Nolan said, "Get in front," his jaw firm.

She crawled over the seat and sat beside him. She was wearing a man's white shirt and tight tan jeans. She wore no shoes and her blond hair was tousled. Coppery nipples were visible beneath the white shirt and Nolan had an urge to take her up on it, to drive straight out of town with her and forget the whole goddamn fucking thing. But it passed.

He said, "Why do you want out of Chelsey?"

Her eyes were wild saucers. "Elliot!" she scream-whispered. "I'm scared of that bastard!"

"Why?"

"I . . . I saw him shoot Broome tonight."

"And he let you go?"

"He didn't see me. I was in the john, hiding."

"What were you doing with Broome? How do you know Elliot?"

Her eyes lowered. "This morning . . . this morning I didn't level with you. This morning . . . I guess that's yesterday by now, isn't it?"

"Skip it. Tell me where you fit into this."

"Well, when you came up to my apartment asking questions about Irene Tisor, I knew you'd be coming. Or might come, at least. Elliot paid me fifty bucks to find out who you were, what you wanted. See I used to be Broome's girl, in a way. And Elliot was Broome's boss. Elliot, the son-of-a-bitch, he even had me over to his place a few times, but he never even touched me. Is he a faggot or something?"

"I don't know. Get back to it."

"Okay. Anyway, Elliot thought you might be around because this guy named Dinneck, know him?"

"We met."

"Well, this Dinneck found my name in a notebook in your motel room or something. And he told Elliot about it and so Elliot told me to find out who you were when you came around . . ."

"All right," Nolan said, making the proper connections.

She swallowed. "I shouldn't tell you this, but . . . but Dinneck was in the can, listening, all that time you were in my apartment at the Arms."

Nolan smiled flatly. "You didn't by any chance hit him in the throat after I left?"

"Why, yes . . . yes I did. Hit him right smack in the adam's apple. The bastard made a pass at me. Why?"

"Never mind," Nolan said, turning the key in the ignition. "I got to find Elliot's house. I know it's on Fairport Drive. You want to tell me where it is exactly, or do I go looking?"

"You won't find it looking."

"Tell me where it is, then."

"You gonna take me along?"

"Why should I?"

"Because you might need some friendly companionship when this is all over."

"Maybe I got that already."

"Not *this* friendly, you don't. Besides, *I* know where Elliot lives."

"All right," Nolan said, "we'll see. Now let's find Elliot's house before he finds us."

"Fairport Drive's in the ritzy section across the river. By Chelsey Park."

Nolan nodded and she directed him there, over the bridge and into the upper class residential district ringing the park.

"That one," she told him, pointing out an imitation Southern Plantation, pillars and all. The whole "Gone With the Wind" route.

Nolan drove past it, parking half a block away.

"Which bedroom is Elliot's?"

"Second story, farthest window to the left."

"He got a den, anything like that?"

"Right under the bedroom on the first floor."

"Good girl." He patted her thigh and lifted her chin until her eyes were level with his. "Sit here and keep your mouth shut. Take this, it's cold." He gave her his parka. "I'm going to leave the car here. If things look bad, call Vicki Trask's apartment and ask for Mitchell."

"Mitchell? Hey, are you a cop?"

"Hell no."

"I didn't think you were. I had an idea you were a gangster or something. Like my daddy."

"Your daddy?"

"Yeah, didn't I mention that? My daddy's name is Gordon, Mr. Webb. One-Thumb Gordon, as his business associates would call him."

"Christ." That was all he needed. Gordon was Charlie's left hand, missing thumb or not.

"Something wrong?"

"You and your father close?"

"Oh, yeah," she said, "just like this." She crossed her first and middle finger. "This is me," first finger, "and this is him," middle finger. She laughed. "Daddy's a bastard, too, just like Elliot."

Nolan patted her thigh again. "We're going to get along fine, Lyn."

She smiled and bobbed her head. Her eyes went wide as he withdrew the .38 from under his arm. "Ditch the car here if you have to go for help," he said. "I saw a phone booth on the other side of the park."

She nodded again and he left her there.

He walked along the sidewalk at a normal rate, passing two other homes, a red brick two-story and a grey stucco, before he reached the would-be Tara, which sat way back in a huge lawn, back at least fifty yards from the street and bordered on both sides by eight-foot hedges. Elliot's place was isolated, a virtual island. The Navy Band could play in the living room and the neighbors wouldn't hear a thing.

Nolan crept along the edge of the high shrubbery. He reached the house and eased along the white walls, looking into each darkened window and finding no signs of life in the house. Past two pillars, past the porch, past two more pillars and on to another row of blackened windows. Finally, when he reached the last window he found that it had been covered with black drapes so that the room would appear dark from the street.

Elliot's den.

The grass rustled behind him; Nolan whirled and swung his .38 like a battle-axe and clipped the guy on the side of the head. He went down like wet cement. He was dressed in a chauffeur's cap and get-up but he looked like a gone-to-seed hood, which upon closer examination was what he proved to be. A major league gunman Nolan had known long ago in Chicago, a gun grown soft and sent out to the minors. Nolan found a house key in the jacket of the chauffeur's uniform.

He walked to the big brass-knockered door, slipped the key in the lock and turned it. He pushed gently and the door yawned open.

He was in a vestibule, a fancy one, for though it was dark, when he leaned against the wall he felt the rich texture of brocade wallpaper. Ahead a few steps he could see light pouring out from under a door. Silently Nolan went to it and ran a hand over the surface. Plywood with a nice veneer, but plywood. Something a man could put his foot through.

He slammed his heel into it and it sprang open like a berserk jack-in-the-box and Nolan dove in, clutching the .38. Immediately he saw a black leather chair and went for cover. But there was no gunfire to greet him, or even an exclamation of surprise.

When Nolan looked out from behind the chair he saw a thin, very pale man in horn-rimmed glasses. The man was standing over a suitcase on a table by the wall, transferring stacks of money from a safe into the suitcase. There was a .38 Smith and Wesson, a twin to Nolan's, on the floor next to the man. The man eyed the gun, his trembling hand extended in mid-air wondering whether or not to try for it.

"No," said Nolan. "Don't even think about it."

The man heaved a defiant sigh and straightened out his blue double-breasted sportscoat from under which peeked an apple-red turtleneck, brushed off his lighter blue slacks. He appeared to be a usually cool-headed type who'd recently lost his cool head. And he was trying to get it back, without much luck.

"Elliot," Nolan said.

"Mr. Webb," he replied. The voice was nervous, even cracking into higher pitch once, but it was the voice of a man determined to regain his dignity.

"I'm not much for talking," Nolan said. "Suppose you just keep packing that suitcase with your money and then hand it over to me."

"And after that you'll kill me?"

Nolan shrugged.

"You don't have a chance, Webb. *Webb!* That's a laugh. You're Nolan, I know you're Nolan, you think the Boys haven't circulated your picture?"

"Pack the fucking suitcase and maybe later we'll have time for an autograph."

Elliot managed a smile, a smile that seemed surprisingly confident. The pieces of his composure were gradually falling back into place. "Your chances of survival, Mr. Nolan, are somewhat limited. You see, it dawned on me this afternoon just who you really were. I wasn't positive, of course, not having seen you, but I didn't want to take any chances. I called Charlie Franco personally. At this very moment—"

Nolan's harsh laugh cut him off like an unpaid light bill. "Who did you call after Charlie? J. Edgar Hoover?"

Elliot's face twitched.

"I got you figured down the line, Elliot. The double-cross you been working on the Boys is going to put you on their shit list, too—right next to me."

"I don't have any idea what you're talking about."

"Okay, Elliot, cut the talk. Back to the money." Nolan gestured with the .38.

Elliot returned to the safe and kept on piling stack after stack of bills into the suitcase. Nolan lit a smoke and sat in the black leather chair.

A few minutes had passed when Elliot looked up from his money stacking and said, "Want to tell me how you got it figured?"

Nolan lifted his shoulders. "The way I see it, you took on this piddling operation for the Boys because at the time you had nothing better to do. If you were already working for the Boys, you might not've had a choice. The job was meant to make George Franco look and feel like a part of the organization. To help save face for the Franco name. And as time went on, you got bored with it, figured a way to make some easy money and retire to a life of luxury."

Nolan leaned forward in the chair, casually keeping the .38 leveled at Elliot. "The Chelsey operation was pulling in pretty good money, for what it was. Money made mostly off college kid pleasures, booze and pep pills and some LSD for the supposed hippies. Bagmen from Chicago came in every six weeks and picked up the profits. Around thirty G, I suppose, for each six week period."

"More like twenty G," Elliot corrected.

"Okay." Nolan's information on that point had come from the initial talk with Sid Tisor, so it figured the take was only twenty G per six weeks. That damn Sid always did exaggerate.

"The thing is," Nolan continued, "you had a prime connection. A musical junkie named Broome who could get the stuff for you. So you decided to break in an extra source of personal revenue—hard narcotics—without telling the Boys about it."

Elliot had the suitcase full now and he closed the lid. "All right, Nolan. I've been directing a little traffic in drugs. You blame me? I was getting table scraps off this set-up. They paid my bills, sure set me up good with this house and everything. But my cut of the 'piddling' action was puny."

"No wonder you got greedy. You make good money from the Chelsey narcotics trade?"

"What do you think? I've been supplying dealers from

cities in three states. There's enough profit to go around, Nolan. You could have a nice cut, too."

Nolan nodded. "One hundred percent *is* a nice cut."

"Don't be a glutton about it. This isn't the Boys' money, it's mine! Your grievance is with the Boys, not with Irwin Elliot! I'm like you, Nolan, out to take the Boys for a ride."

Nolan shook his head no. "Forget it. You're *part* of the Boys. Maybe you're worse."

"We could be partners . . ."

"Hey, I put nothing past you, not after you wasted your three partners tonight."

"No. Dinneck and Tulip did that—"

"Dinneck and Tulip got banged up earlier tonight. They didn't kill Saunders, Broome and George. You did. Three murders in one night, a gentleman like you. And just to clean house. What's the world coming to?"

Elliot's laugh was almost a cackle. "You're amusing, Nolan, you really are. Yes, I murdered those morons tonight. When the Boys find out three of their Chelsey men were murdered with a .38 and that Nolan was in town, they'll blame *you*, not Irwin Elliot. And when they find out I've vacated the premises, they'll assume I was just frightened of what you'd do to me. By the time they figure out what was really going on in Chelsey, I'll be in South America."

"I don't think so," Nolan said. "Hand me the suitcase. And no fun and games."

Elliot scowled, tossed the suitcase at Nolan's feet.

"How much is there, Elliot?"

"Near a quarter million dollars."

"Not bad. How long you been planning this?"

"Long enough. I knew all along I'd have to get out sooner or later, because once the Commission got wind of narcotics action they hadn't sanctioned, I'd be a marked man. I wanted to wait near the end of a six week period so I'd have the Boys' twenty thousand take, too. And it took me a while to liquidate my stocks and bonds . . . I don't keep this much in cash on hand all the time, you know."

"You're not stupid, Elliot," Nolan said, "just not smart. You got the Boys who'll be after you. New York'll want your hide. And the feds will want a piece, too. You're going to be a popular boy. I'm considering not killing you. It might be fun to tie you up and leave you here and let everybody fight over you."

A voice from behind them boomed, "Drop the gun, Webb, will ya drop it now?"

Nolan turned and saw a very battered Tulip standing in the doorway of the den, holding a .45 with an incredibly steady hand.

"*Now,* Webb."

Nolan let the gun plop to the soft carpet.

"All right, you fucker . . . I got a score to settle with you."

Tulip's six foot frame lumbered over to him, the arm Nolan had wounded earlier hanging limp as a dead tree limb, brown with dried blood. Nolan couldn't tell if Tulip had ever gotten that shot of H he'd needed so badly hours before; all Nolan knew was that Tulip seemed in full control as he raised his good arm and aimed the .45 at Nolan's head.

There was a blur of movement in the doorway and a familiar voice cried, "Tulip! Stop, Tulip, it's me!"

Tulip smiled, turned away from Nolan and faced the door.

The slug caught Tulip in the stomach, hard, and Tulip lay down like a hibernating bear. He looked up at the smoking nine millimeter in the hand of Dinneck and said, "What the hell did you do that for?" Then Tulip closed his eyes and stopped breathing.

"Thanks," Nolan said.

"Saving your life wasn't the point," Dinneck said. "But Tulip was Elliot's man, and I needed him out of the way." This he said even as he stepped over the big dead man.

"Allow me to introduce myself, gents. My name *is* Dinneck, but you also have the right, I think, to know who I represent."

Dinneck sat down on a black leather couch and let the nine millimeter take turns staring at Nolan and Elliot.

"I'm a native New Yorker," he said, and coughed, his throat raspy. "My employers heard some rumors about dope traffic in this part of the country. Around Chelsey to be exact."

Dinneck rose, stepping over the corpse of his ex-partner.

"I work for the Commission."

4

"Won't you sit down, Mr. Webb?" Dinneck asked, his hoarse voice dripping sarcasm. "I have some business to take care of with Mr. Elliot here, before you and I settle our personal differences."

Nolan said, "Your ball game," and sat back down in the black leather chair. The gun Elliot had dropped at Nolan's command a few minutes before lay unseen behind the closed suitcase of money. Elliot seemed to have forgotten it, and Dinneck didn't know about it. Nolan would make his move for the .38, but not yet. Dinneck was in the mood to talk, so Nolan would listen and watch while he waited for the right moment to move.

Dinneck stroked his throat, which was visibly bruised from both Lyn Parks' assault and Nolan's blows of earlier that evening. He looked weak, he looked pale—almost as pale as Elliot.

"Mr. Elliot," Dinneck was saying, "I was assigned to you by my employers to work undercover until I had enough on you to be convinced positively of your guilt. Which I am. I placed a long-distance call this afternoon to a gentleman in New York who gave me instructions as to what to do about you. You see, my employers don't take it kindly when somebody opens up a business without a franchise."

"You never saw a thing," Elliot snapped. "You weren't

involved with the narcotics operation at all. None of the men the Boys sent me were."

"That's right. You used me for strong-arm work. Beat people up, pressure them. Like I did with that reporter, Davis, who skipped town. Watched over people, like Mr. Franco . . . the late Mr. Franco, now, I hear. And Broome and Saunders, too. My, my, but you were a busy little fella tonight. Yes, I ran your errands, and you were careful to keep me away from your narcotics set-up. Instinct maybe." Dinneck coughed, caressing his throat; talking was obviously painful to him, but he couldn't resist. He coughed again and glanced pointedly at Nolan, who sat motionless, silent, like an obedient school-boy. Then he returned his gaze to Elliot.

"You got to remember Chelsey's a small town, Mr. Elliot," Dinneck said. "Junkies and pushers aren't hard to pick out in a town this size. And the college punks have big mouths, like to brag about getting their kicks. Your bosom pal Broome was a pusher and a junkie both, he could've worn a sign it was so obvious. And my own late partner, here, was paying half his salary back to put in his arm."

Sweat was streaming down Elliot's face; his confident tones turned back into the high-pitched squeaking he'd used when Nolan first came into the den. "There's a quarter million in that suitcase, Dinneck! Take it and let me go. I'll never say a word."

Dinneck smiled. "You don't cross the Commission and live, Elliot. If I did that, even if I killed you and kept the money, my life'd be as worthless as . . . as yours."

Elliot was shaking his head no as Dinneck brought up the nine-millimeter; then Elliot remembered something. "Nolan," he said, "you don't know he's Nolan!"

Dinneck hesitated. He lowered the nine-millimeter, puzzled. "Nolan? What the hell are you talking about? What is he talking about, Webb?"

"Search me," Nolan said.

"He isn't Webb, he's Nolan," Elliot spewed. "There's a quarter million on his head."

"We got quarter millions up the ass tonight," Nolan said.

Dinneck coughed, covering his mouth with his hand. "Shut up, Webb . . ." He coughed, coughed again. "Okay, Elliot, okay. This guy here, this Webb, he's Nolan? The guy that resigned the outfit by shooting one of the Francos?"

Elliot nodded and didn't stop nodding. "That's him, he's the one, a quarter million dollars."

Dinneck gave them both a broad, toothy smile. "That's nice to know, children—that's real comforting to know."

"Look, I told you and I didn't have to," Elliot said, his eyes filled with desperation. "Give me a break. Don't kill me, don't shoot me."

"I'm not going to shoot you, friend," Dinneck told him. "Not with a gun anyway." He motioned Elliot up against the wall.

Nolan leaned back in the chair. He had a good idea of what would be coming next; he'd heard rumors of this practice among mob enforcers when he'd been working for the Boys. He eyed the .38 and knew it wasn't time to move. Not yet.

Dinneck reached into his pocket and withdrew a brown carrying case about the size of a small picture frame. He snapped it open and the light of the room caught the reflection from the tip of the hypodermic needle within the case and tossed it around.

"You a user, Elliot? You take the stuff yourself, or do you just sell it?"

"I'm no user, you know that. And I don't smoke or drink or womanize, either."

"Well good for you. You're just all virtue and no vice, aren't you?"

Nolan said, "Get it over with."

Dinneck said, "Don't be so anxious, dead man. Your turn'll come soon enough." He walked over to Elliot, shoved him hard against the wall, then held the hypo up and said, "You ever hear of a mainliner?"

Elliot didn't answer.

"Of course you have. You're in the business, aren't you? A mainliner is a shot of H, right in the old blood-stream. Into a nice fat juicy vein. My employers are of the opinion that a person dealing in drugs ought to get first hand view of what he's selling. Now that's only good business, isn't it?"

Elliot plastered himself against the wall. "You . . . you're going to give me an overdose! You're going to kill me with that thing!"

Dinneck nodded. "And the cops will find a poor slob who just misjudged and popped too big a cap for his own good."

Elliot began to scream and Dinneck slammed his fist into the man's temple. Elliot slid to the floor and lay there, a puddle of flesh.

Dinneck took a rubber strap from one of his coat pockets, kneeled over, bared Elliot's right arm and tied the strap around it. The hypo was already loaded and it was no trouble for Dinneck to jam the needle into a throbbing, bulging vein and press his thumb down on the plunger.

Nolan leaned over, ready to go for the .38 that waited for him of the floor a few feet away. Dinneck caught the motion from the corner of his eye and sank his heel into Nolan's hand just before it had reached the gun. Then he kicked the .38 across the room, at the same time back-handing Nolan, who flopped back in the chair and waited for a second chance that would probably never come.

Elliot was semi-conscious, crying softly and spasmodically. Dinneck kicked Elliot's head once and put him out.

"He won't be waking up," Nolan said.

Dinneck tossed the hypo to the soft carpet. "Not in this world."

"How much did you have in the hypo?"

"Enough. Enough horse to kill a horse. Hah, horse, hell, a herd." Dinneck laughed some more, but the laughter turned into a racking cough.

Nolan thought, keep coughing, pal, come on, got to make another try for you.

"My eastern employers didn't pay me to kill you, Nolan, but somehow I don't think they'll mind. You're a thorn in the Boys' side, and the Boys are part of the Commission, after all." Dinneck slipped his free hand into his coat pocket and popped a toothpick into the corner of his mouth. "Besides, I can use the money. Quarter million's gonna go a long way. It'll hurt, you know, handing in Elliot's suitcase of bills."

"I didn't figure you killed for free."

Dinneck hefted the .38. "You got a point. I'm strictly a contract man, and all my contract work's done for the Commission. A loyal soldier. But in your case, I'd make an exception, even if there wasn't a quarter million on your head."

"You talk too much, Dinneck," Nolan said, "for a man with a sore throat."

Dinneck grinned. "Two-hundred fifty G's is gonna soothe that fine."

The nine-millimeter came up and faced Nolan, and Nolan knew his move had to be fast and good and now . . .

The shot came from the doorway, a thunderclap that couldn't happen, slamming into the wall between them.

Mitchell stood in the doorway, a Police Special smoking in his fist. "Hold it right there!"

But Dinneck didn't do anything of the kind.

He whirled and dropped to one knee, bringing up the .38 to try to blast Mitchell out of the door. Nolan heaved the suitcase of money at Dinneck's hand, knocked the automatic flying, and the mouth of the suitcase jumped open and vomited bills. Nolan sliced through the drifting green bills and drew his foot back to kick in Dinneck's head. Dinneck, scrambling after the nine-millimeter, saw Nolan's foot coming and grabbed it and spun Nolan around and threw him over on his back. Mitchell was still in the door, forced to hold fire because of all the movement.

Nolan landed hard, on his own .38, where it had been kicked away by Dinneck minutes earlier. Nolan rolled over, scooped it up and looked up into Dinneck's face and Dinneck's gun.

Nolan squeezed off a single shot, then rolled away, ready to squeeze off another. But it wasn't necessary.

The slug had caught Dinneck in the throat, and the small blue hole that marked its entry appeared just under the man's adam's apple. The nine-millimeter tumbled from his hand, and Dinneck did a half-turn and crashed to the floor. He used his last few seconds foolishly; he tried to speak, dredging up nothing except blood, and he tried to grasp the gun, coming up with a wad of money that wouldn't be buying him anything. His mouth went slack, the toothpick fell away from his lips, and he didn't have time to close his eyes before he died.

Nolan looked at Mitchell, standing there in the doorway with the Police Special in his hand; cordite-smell was in the air.

Nolan said, "Talk about cavalry," but Mitchell didn't react. Nolan shrugged and started picking up the scattered cash that lay over, under and around the lifeless bodies.

It took ten minutes to repack the suitcase.

5

Mitchell had come alone. At Vicki Trask's he'd gotten a call from Lyn Parks saying she'd seen several of Elliot's men go into the house, and Nolan would probably need help.

Now Nolan and Mitchell stood in the hall outside the den where the remains of Elliot, Tulip and Dinneck were inside waiting for Chelsey's harried medical examiner. The chauffeur Nolan had clubbed over the head less than an hour before sat handcuffed and dazed in the den with the dead men. Since Mitchell was the only cop who'd reached the scene so far, Nolan was anxious to be on his way.

"I'm keeping the suitcase of money," Nolan said flatly.

Mitchell didn't say anything. He looked beat. He'd been up most of the night and in eleven years of police work had never run across an evening that remotely compared to this one. He was shaking his head and gazing in at the three bodies in the den.

Nolan watched the cop, who seemed practically in shock. Nolan said, "Mitchell, we made a deal. I want your word you'll keep me out of this. Just cover up the incident as best you can."

Mitchell nodded, his eyes a pair of burnt-out holes. "Okay," he conceded. "But you got to get out as soon as possible. I don't want anybody finding out I opened the door for this massacre."

"I'll need an hour," Nolan said.

Mitchell said, "Okay, okay," not giving a damn, and stood looking into the den.

Neither man said a word as Nolan left, suitcase in hand.

When he reached the car he was met by a bubbling Lyn Parks. He let her talk, reaching an arm in the open window and grabbing the keys from the ignition. He ignored her eager interrogation and opened the trunk and stowed away the suitcase of bills, where it lay innocently with the rest of his luggage, just another piece of baggage. He got back in the car, started it and headed for Vicki Trask's apartment, paying no attention to his talkative passenger.

He pulled up in front of the apartment and got out of the Lincoln. Looking in at Lyn Parks he said, "We'll have plenty of time for talk later. You got a car?"

"Yeah, but . . ."

"What is it?"

"An ancient Plymouth, why?"

"Walking distance?"

"Yeah, as a matter of fact it's in a parking lot over by the Arms. Couple, maybe three blocks."

"Ever been to Wisconsin?"

"No, but . . ."

He tossed a ten dollar bill in her lap. "If you want to go to Wisconsin with me, go get your car and fill it with gas. Drive it back here and wait for me. If you don't want to go with me, don't be here when I get back."

Nolan left her before she could say anything else and opened the door in the middle of Chelsey Ford Sales. He went up the flight of stairs that led to Vicki's apartment and knocked once. She came to the door, smiling in relief at the sight of him and throwing her arms around him.

He broke her warm clasp and led her to the couch. He told her to sit and she did.

Nolan went back and closed the door. He looked at her. She seemed tired but was still very nice to look at. He remembered how she'd been in bed.

"Like I said before, I got nothing personal in this," Nolan said. "We slept together once and I like you, but it ends there."

There was horror in her face. "What are you talking about, Earl?"

"Go ahead and call me Nolan. I haven't figured out yet what I'll be calling you."

"You'll keep calling me Vicki, of course! What are you talking about, what's wrong?"

Nolan stood over her and looked down. "I owed Sid Tisor a debt. So to pay it back to him I came to Chelsey to look into his daughter's death. If it was murder, he would as soon I kill the murderer. If suicide, or an accident, I was supposed to confirm it with him and let it go at that."

"Why are you going over all this past history?"

"Be quiet." Nolan let a cigarette, the last of the pack. He crumpled it and tossed it on the table and went on. "My first thought was to look into Chelsey's branch of the Outfit. As it turned out, the Boys didn't have anything to do with Irene Tisor. Other than indirectly, sell the initial cube of LSD she took that night."

"Isn't that where you were? Having it out with the criminals and all? Isn't your debt paid?"

"I had it out with the 'criminals,' all right. Three more died, died before I could ask them what they knew about Irene Tisor. But I didn't have to ask, because they didn't know anything. No, Vicki, the debt isn't paid."

"What are you talking about? Why are you telling me all

this, Nolan—I really want to know!"

"Maybe you should be doing the telling," he said. "Maybe you'll tell me what's going on here."

"Nothing's going on here!"

Nolan said, "You could start by telling me how the real Vicki Trask died, Irene."

She looked up, slowly, and saw in his face, in the ice-grey of his eyes, that he knew the truth, at least partially. Her mouth jerked spasmodically and she brought up her hands, cupping them over her face to catch the tears.

Nolan spoke softly. "It took a long time to recognize you, Irene."

She glared at him wildly, her eyes red, her face streaked with tears. "How . . . how did you know?"

"It was hard," he told her. "Your hair is different now. And you had your nose fixed. Your father told me about that, I should have remembered. And when I saw you last you were a child. Not a woman."

"When . . . *when* did you know?"

"Tonight in bed I figured it. But I must've suspected all along. You couldn't resist calling me Nolan, could you? You had to play a game with me."

"It wasn't really a game," she said, beginning to regain control. "I did idolize you, Nolan, as a child and a teen-ager and even now. But since I was playing Vicki Trask, I couldn't recognize you first-hand."

"Why, Irene? Why did you play Vicki Trask? Why does everyone who knows you in Chelsey know you as Vicki Trask? Why did everyone in Chelsey think the real Vicki Trask was Irene Tisor? And why is the false-Irene/real-Vicki dead?"

The tears began again, and Nolan waited for them to stop. Then he said, "Tell it, Irene."

She nodded, swallowing the hard lump in her throat and rubbing her red eyes with balled fists.

She said, "Before I left home for college, my father had one of his infrequent heart-to-heart talks with me. He told me . . . told me that before he'd retired, he'd been involved with organized crime. Our whole family was, on my mother's side. That he had been involved for more than twenty years."

She stopped and Nolan said, "So?"

"I was . . . was ashamed. Oh, I know, I should have guessed what kind of business he was in. If from nothing else, from the kind of people who showed up now and then at the house. People like you, Nolan. But . . . but he was such a mild man, a gentle person . . . it really threw me to find out he'd been a . . . a criminal. I'd always thought of him as so upright . . . it suddenly disgusted, revolted me . . . with him, myself, my whole life!"

She hesitated again, but Nolan prodded her and she resumed.

"I wanted to be respectable. It made me feel . . . feel dirty, somehow. A dirt I *had* to wash off. He was my parent, my only parent, since my mother died when I was born. And now, I . . . I just wanted to start over. So I decided to go to Chelsey and on the bus I struck up an acquaintance with a girl, a girl who was headed for Chelsey herself. Vicki Trask."

"Go on."

"Vicki looked something like me, and we had similar interests. She wanted to go to college and study art, but her parents were both dead and left her without a penny. And her grades weren't strong enough to get her a scholarship. I . . . I didn't care about college any more . . . I just wanted an anonymous life, away from my father. But I still wanted my father's monthly allowance—I felt he owed me that much. It was Vicki who got the idea . . . the idea to switch names and everything. She could go to college, and I could keep getting checks from daddy to underwrite my college-girl existence. It sounded like it might work, and if it didn't, the worst that could happen was she could be kicked out of a school and I could be fired from a job. Well, it did work. We made a pact. We set it up together, got this apartment and all and traded identities. It took some doing, but we managed to shuffle some papers around and fix some documents and . . . and just swap places."

Nolan stabbed out the cigarette. "Why didn't you just get married if you wanted to change your goddamn name?"

"It . . . it was a *mental* thing with me . . . and I wasn't ready for a man in my life. Nolan, you were the first man I'd been with since I came to Chelsey."

Nolan shook his head, said, "Okay. Go ahead and tell the rest."

"Well, everything worked out pretty well. It wasn't hard for me to get a job in a small town like this without anybody checking the references too close. Though I was kind of scared, since it was a bank I'd applied to, and I figured they might be careful about who they hired. But they didn't spot anything false in my references and I've been working there ever since."

Nolan said, "Yeah, I can believe it." He knew a lot of banks picked girls on a basis of looks and personality; he just hoped they were more cautious in the banks *his* money was stored in. He said, "Keep talking."

She stared at the floor, avoiding Nolan's eyes. "And . . . and my father . . . I loved him so much, once . . . respected him . . . but the love was transformed into hate, when I found out what he *really* was."

"Cover some new ground," he told her, seeing the first light of the sun coming in through the loft windows above them.

"What . . . what's left to tell?"

"Quit stalling. How did your roommate die?"

She tried to speak but her throat caught. The tears began again, in a violent rush. Nolan grabbed her by the shoulders, shook her. "How? How did it happen? Did you kill her?"

She bit the ends of her fingers. "I . . . I don't know . . . I don't suppose I'll ever know."

Nolan released her. "Calm down and tell me about it."

She leaned forward. "Remember what I told you about Irene Tisor? The false one, I mean, before you knew? How she was getting wild the last few months? That was true, even though I was talking about the other Irene. She started to abuse our agreement, feeling a strange sort of freedom, I guess, from living under another person's name. I began to feel . . . to feel I had to end the farce . . . take the name back and forget my pride and leave Chelsey, go somewhere, anywhere else! Anywhere but Chelsey! As long as these pseudo-hippie friends of Irene's weren't around." She laughed. "I get confused, even now. Who's Vicki? Who's Irene? Which am I?"

"What happened?"

"She wanted to try LSD. Grass wasn't enough for her, yet she was afraid of anything stronger. Except LSD. She read a lot of books, magazine articles on it . . . some of her weird friends were urging her to give it a try. When she finally got the nerve, she got this little sugar cube, from that Broome character, she said. It was wrapped in cellophane, like a piece of candy. She brought it to the apartment and told me about how she was going to try it and said she needed my help. Either I gave her a hand with it, or she'd call my father on the phone and expose me. What she needed was a guide, a person to be with her when she was on the stuff who would make sure nothing . . . nothing *bad* happened . . . while she was on the trip, you know? I said I'd do it."

Nolan sat down next to her, steadied her with a hand on her shoulder.

Her voice trembled; it was soft, distant, as she recalled an evening she'd tried to forget.

"We started out in the apartment," she said. "She ran around the room looking at things, feeling, eating, tasting, touching. She was an animal, writhing on the floor, a serpent, utterly stripped of any inhibitions she'd ever felt. She told me it was wonderful, she could feel and taste and hear and see all at once, never as before. She . . . she seemed almost insane, and it got worse . . . worse as she went along. Then she sat in a chair . . . that chair, the chair right across from us now . . . and had a conversation with someone only she could see. Claimed it . . . it was her soul. Then she sprang out of the chair and ran down the steps. I followed her . . . I didn't try to stop her, there was no reasoning with her . . . it was late and no one was around to bother us."

She hesitated, buried her eyes in her hands and said, "She came to . . . to that building. Twill Building. She pulled down a fire escape and she climbed it . . . climbed up, up to the top . . . and I followed her. She said . . . said she wanted to taste the stars, feel the sky. She got on the roof-top and . . . and she ran . . . ran around like a crazy woman . . . and chattered about God, how she was meeting God . . . and I snapped. I couldn't stand it any more. I grabbed her, tried to shake her, shake her out of it . . . but no use. No use. She was strong . . . she fought me . . . we scuffled around . . . tumbled . . . rolled . . . and suddenly the edge of the building was there and we kept struggling and . . . and she just . . . she just went over. She went over, that's all."

There was silence in the room for a moment, then she said, "I got away without a single person seeing me. I came back here and went to bed, but I didn't sleep. The next day, Irene Tisor was dead. When I saw the word would get back to my father that his daughter was dead . . . I let it ride. I let it ride."

Nolan stood up. "I see."

She reached out for him, her eyes dry but still bloodshot. "I don't think I . . . I pushed her, Nolan, but . . . I don't know."

"Sure."

"What . . . what will you tell my father?"

He shrugged. "The truth, maybe. Or perhaps that his daughter *is* dead and to forget it. I don't know yet."

"Do you think I . . . I killed her? On purpose, I mean?"

"I don't know," Nolan said. "Maybe I don't even give a damn. But any way you spell it, I can't scrape up much pity for you."

"Nolan . . ."

"You condemned your father for being a criminal, then turned around and made a lie of your own life. You slept with me, a thief, a killer ten times over. And maybe you even killed somebody yourself."

The tears were back again. Funny how Nolan had told Sid Tisor when the thing began that it was the living to feel sorry for, and not the dead. Sid had mourned the living all along.

"Your father worked for the Outfit, all right," he said. "But he was a pencil jockey, a book man. Maybe just being a part of the Outfit makes you a criminal, but Sid sure didn't share any love for his bosses. Helping me like he did proves that."

She kept crying but Nolan didn't pay any attention.

"You took the good life on a platter from him," Nolan said, "kept it, and threw him away."

"What can I do, Nolan?"

"That's your problem."

"But Nolan . . ."

"My debt's paid. Kiss Chelsey goodbye for me."

"Don't leave! Tell me what to do! What should I do, Nolan, tell me!"

"You should probably go to hell," he said. "But you want my advice so bad, I'll give it. Become Irene Tisor again. Drop the Vicki Trask tag and start over. But quietly, or they'll trace you back to the death of your roommate."

"But they'll find out, won't they?"

"I don't think so. The death of Irene Tisor is a closed case. It's marked probable suicide in a file. But stick around Chelsey and your chances aren't so good. The easy days in this town are over what with the Boys not having an operation here any more and the on-the-take police chief dead."

"How? How can I do it?"

Nolan reached in his pocket and dangled the keys of the Lincoln in front of her. "These keys fit the car I been driving around Chelsey. It's rented in your father's name. The car, with the keys in it, will be waiting at the bottom of the steps for you. When you're ready, drive it back to Peoria."

Her eyes were red, wet circles. "What do you mean?"

"I mean go back to your father. Go back where they know you and you can explain your 'death' by saying it was a mix-up and they'll believe you. Your father's a lonely old guy. Just be careful you don't give him a heart attack when you show up. He'll be so happy to find you alive he won't give a damn about what an ungrateful little bitch you've been."

"Go back to him?"

"If he'll have you."

"But . . ."

Nolan turned and walked to the door. "Give Sid my regards. And tell him we're even."

She swallowed and said, "Maybe I'll . . . I'll do that."

He opened the door. "So long, Vicki . . . or Irene." His lips formed the humorless line she'd come to know as his smile. "Maybe I'll stop by Peoria in a year or so," he said. "And see who you are."

He closed the door and left her.

6

It was a red Plymouth that was dirty as hell and hadn't been new for twelve years. Lyn Parks was sitting behind the wheel, her long blonde hair hanging down over the shoulders of Nolan's parka, which she still wore. The Plymouth's engine was running, the muffler sounding as if it had seconds to live.

"Well?" she called, as Nolan came from the doorway of the apartment.

"Well?" he returned, heading for the Lincoln. He opened up the trunk of the big car, got out his clothes-bags, luggage and the money-stuffed suitcase. He slammed the lid back down, tossed the keys in the open window of the Lincoln and joined Lyn Parks in the dirty red Plymouth, piling the back seat with his baggage.

"You need all that crap?" she asked.

He patted the suitcase of cash fondly. "This one's all I really need."

"What am I supposed to do?"

"Drive."

"Where?"

"Think you can find Milwaukee?"

"Eventually," she shrugged.

"I got a stop to make." Nolan's Milwaukee contact, a broker named Richmond, would see that the quarter million was properly banked/invested.

"You're the boss," she said. "I just hope this crate'll make it as far as Wisconsin."

"I'll buy you a new one on the way."

She grinned. "Sounds good." She started the car, her blond hair bouncing, and four minutes later Chelsey was a memory.

Nolan leaned back, his hand on Lyn Parks' thigh. There would be no sweat from the Boys for a while; they'd be busy trying to figure out what had been going on in Chelsey. And that was good, he hadn't relaxed for months. He squeezed Lyn's thigh, leaned his head back and shut his eyes. Wisconsin would be cold this time of year. It would be nice to have a bed warmer.